The
Tree
of
Idleness

BarbarianSpy

www.barbarianspy.com

This book is copyright © Shabbu 2010
Shabbu asserts his right to be known as the author of this work.
Second edition published by BarbarianSpy in 2010.
Cover design by S Bush © 2010
Cover Photo ©123rf.com
ISBN ebook 978-1-921879-23-4
ISBN Print : 978-1-922187-82-6
All rights reserved.

BarbarianSpy
Jindalee St
Toronto, NSW 2283
Australia

The

Tree of Idleness

or

The Villa's Curse

by

Shabbu

CONTENTS

Preface   7

Chapter 1: Almalfi Possession   9

Chapter 2: Kent Possession   21

Chapter 3: Secret Possession   35

Chapter 4: Henson Possession   43

Chapter 5: Munro Possession   57

Chapter 6: Taylor Possession   73

Chapter 7: Kessel Possession   85

Chapter 8: Broken Possession   101

Chapter 9: Vincent Possession   121

Authors' Notes   127

About the Authors   129

Preface

For fifty years men come to the island of Cyprus, a Mediterranean paradise split and war torn by a marathon ethnic struggle between Greek and Turk, each consciously seeking connection with the writings of the British novelist and essayist Lawrence Durrell. They all take up tenancy, some longer than others, in the Bellapais villa where Durrell wrote his masterpiece, *The Alexandria Quartet*, and where their landlady is rumored to be the model for one of the central characters in Durrell's love epic. But unconsciously the men come seeking or enticed by something else entirely, pulled by their own desires and by the whisperings of the villa itself down to the Tree of Idleness café on the Bellapais square. To ogle and, in turn, be ogled by the young Turkish Cypriot men there—and to take those men back to the villa for hours of unfettered, wanton pleasure, oblivious to any threat of personal damage or to the rending of the delicate balance of the island's social structure.

The first of the villa's visitors comes in a desperate bid to hold onto a relationship and finds in Bellapais exactly what he was escaping—and chronicles his defeat in a novel that then becomes the foundation and prophetic context for each succeeding tenant, who succumbs, some more willingly and consciously than others, to the lure of the young Turkish Cypriot men in the Tree of Idleness café.

And it is not only the foreign visitors to Bellapais who are affected by the enticement woven by the Bellapais villa. The local men, as well, the young—and maturing and aging—men in the Tree of Idleness café are caught up in the constantly reweaving web of desire and wanton lust, island sexual customs, and doomed relationships.

Just when it appears that the villa is willing to put the cycle to rest, to offer solace to those who have found each other again and chosen constancy over wantonness, the villa's enticing whisperings of the delights of the Tree of Idleness café down on the Bellapais square begin anew.

Chapter 1: Almalfi Possession

by habu

Ahh, the days of drifting down to the Tree of Idleness in the square in the late afternoon and sitting ogling the local Turkish Cypriot men and letting them ogle me until I got that certain look from one I fancied. Then taking him up to my rented villa and letting him vigorously, joyously, and noisily fuck my brains out on a lounger under the sun on the terrace overlooking the Mediterranean.

I laid the pen down. The house on the hill at Bellapais overlooking the Mediterranean below, the sea unseen in the dark of night, but heard in the constant lapping of the waters on the rocky shore, was quiet. Or was it? It seemed to be whispering to me again, compelling me to write what I had written when I intended to be writing something entirely different.

The light of the lamp on the desk was dimming, evidence of the perpetual power problems of the archaic Cypriot electrical plant, I wondered, or some act of sabotage by either the Greek or Turkish side in what was shaping up to be civil war—in some far distant future, I hoped. The shadows cast in the room almost took human shape. How many had sat at this desk before me in this village house where, in the mid 1950s, less than a decade earlier, Lawrence Durrell penned much of his *Alexandria Quartet*—trying to channel his rich prose into their own fingertips?

Had they heard the same whispers I heard? Or was this my personal torment? Uncontrollably torn between two impulses, two lives that could not cohabit. Here because I had made a decision, taken a stand, declared renunciation of a fetish, but torn, drawn to defeat, by the spirit of this house, as evidenced in what I was compelled to write—and then, I was afraid, quite possibly to act out.

I rose from the carved pine chair and tread quietly across the Turkish carpet, seeking the painting in the studio carved out of the far end of the large room, checking to see if he had finished it. Wanting him to finish it, returning it to what it originally had been and then finishing it, a completed painting somehow being the signal of my release from that other impulse.

No. There I was, staring out of the canvas in our never-ending reverie at the café table, perpetually lifting my wine glass in salute to—what was supposed to be him. But only rough sketchings on glaring white canvas where my body faded toward the lower edge and merely a placeholder for him now—although at one time, back in England, his figure had been developing in the painting as well. The completed background of the canvas, incongruously, but perhaps prophetically a sun-drenched deep-ochre-painted rough stone wall. When I had sat for him, I was backed by a rose-laced white-lattice pavilion wall at his father's English country estate. But he had said he saw us in the Mediterranean—and here, in fact we were, on a Mediterranean island.

I had thought he had worked on it today, but when I approached, I saw that the canvas remained unfinished at its foundation. He hadn't wanted to tell me, or so it seemed. But back in London, when he had given me the choice—no, the ultimatum—I watched him wash his own developing figure out of the composition in anger and frustration and he had blurted out that the painting would not be complete again until he could be sure of me.

And when would that be, I wondered. Certainly not tonight. Not with what the spirits of this house had compelled me to ink on the paper this evening. I was drawn back to the desk, and I sat, reluctantly, once again, and picked up the pen and let my hand write what it would—or what the four walls of this room were compelling me to write. I am so, so weak.

And then back down to the square in the twilight after dinner with those fairy lights in the olive trees around the fringe of the stone café terrace, and, in that soft light and twittering laughter of the Mediterranean men and wisps of strong Turkish tobacco drifting up, eyeing and being eyed until I got the certain look from one I fancied and took him back up to the villa and let him fuck me in long, slow, sweeping strokes on the terrace under the stars.

"Mark, it's late. Come to bed, love."

Val's voice, thick and distant with the edge of sleep, intruded as if from the other side of the murmuring sea. Struck with guilt, my hand dropped the pen. I rose once again and moved to the door into the bedroom Val and I shared, a room jutting out on the cliffside terrace toward the sea, with open windows on three sides to the night breezes and the sound of the waves crashing on the rocks far below.

The old, iron bed in the center of the room on wall-to-wall straw matting. A fire still smoldering in the fireplace on the wall adjoining the main wing of the house. Val, naked, and beautifully stretched out in the center of the bed.

I moved to the bed and sat down and laid my hand on the belly of my young lover. Lord Cramner. Such a heady title for the slender, willowy young man who had stolen my heart. Valery Cramner to those not impressed with titles. My darling Val to me. Brilliant, sensitive, artistic, and high strung when awake and in his element with paint brush and oil pallet in his sensuous hands. But vulnerable and young and beckoning now in repose. A smile stealing across his face now, as he felt the heat of my palm on his belly, his eyes still closed. A lock of his curly, shoulder-length, soft-brown hair fell across his face, and I moved my free hand to brush it out of his eyes.

Val took my hand in his and raised it to his lips. He kissed the fingertips and then took the index finger between his full lips and gave languid suck. His eyes still closed, he was only half awake, but this was when he wanted me the most.

I pulled my hand back and stood by the bed. As he turned onto his belly with a sigh, knowing what came next, wanting it, I undid the sash of my robe and let the garment fall off my shoulders and to the floor. I sat on the bed again, this time below his thighs and I leaned my face down, and as I parted his pert, smooth-skinned orbs, I moved my lips and tongue to his puckered, warm entrance.

Val sighed for me as I gently rimmed him, preparing him; he moaned and moved his hips when I entered him with lubricated fingers; he purred when I stretched my body along his back and encased his thighs closely in mine; he cried out softly as I buried my lips in the hollow of his neck and began sliding my cock inside his channel; he groaned and slowly churned his hips. And he turned his head, eyes still closed, to capture my lips with his as I slowly but relentless moved in and out, ever deeper, inside him.

He writhed under me as I mastered him, the older man taking the younger lover, ever deeper and lust-induced thicker, with ever more forceful thrustings. His eyes opened and his back arched against my heaving chest as he spread his seed on the sheeting of the bed. And then he just collapsed into himself, closed his eyes again, and murmured endearments and encouragement as I reached my own climax.

When I felt his breathing had become regular and relaxed, I gently withdrew from him, rose and moved, naked, and now tumescent, back to the desk in the other room. I sat and lifted up the pen with one hand. The other hand glided down my belly, through my pubic bush, and into my lap.

And maybe, if he was really, really beautiful and masterful, taking him back to my bed for a night of sleep broken by brief periods of wanton lust, waking to the feel of a hot poker at my hole and a wheedling whisper for permission at my ear and arching back to accept the homage of a throbbing need to be deep inside me. Breakfasting on the terrace by the small pool and then pulling him into the pool and wrapping my legs around his waist and letting the swirling water soften the rhythmic in and outing as I threw my head back and watched the morning Mediterranean light filter through the sighing branches of the olive trees and thought about my late afternoon visit to the Tree of Idleness café on the Bellapais square, already assessing which eyes I would respond to today.

The pen dropped. I was stroking myself, close once more to ejaculation. Uncontrollably torn between my young lover and his ultimatum and my weak-willed instincts. Having everything I would ever need in him; but my racing mind—and now the spirits of this house, of this jaded village of Bellapais—telling me that there was more than that and that I wanted it. My breathing heavy, my hand working my cock, my mind wandering to the men I'd seen in the open-air café in the Bellapais square just down the winding, uneven cobble-stoned narrow street winding down from this ledge into the Byzantine abbey forecourt.

Searching the young, masculine Turkish men's faces in my mind, seeing their interest. Straining my ears to hear their late-night banter and the sound of the stringed baglama above the crashing of the surf far down the cliffside. Imagining them coming for me, fucking me on the chaise lounge on the terrace by the pool overlooking the blue Mediterranean. Throwing my head back, groaning, twitching, lurching, and then going dormant, collapsing back into the carved pine chair at the writing desk. Once more losing the struggle. Once more betraying my young lover.

* * * *

I wondered if Lawrence Durrell had known the deck was being stacked against us when he offered up this refuge, his own retreat for writing, in northern Cyprus, far from the London swirl, with its distractions and damnations, when Val had decided that we must flee or part. I wonder if the house had tried to pull Durrell down to the intoxicating, devouring men at the café in the Bellapais square as well when he was writing his *Alexandria Quartet* here. When that possibility occurred to me, I poured over my copy of the *Quartet*, looking for evidence, but, as broodingly sexual and sensuous as that master work was, I saw no indication of this in his writing. Perhaps it was just me. Perhaps the house preyed on my weakness alone—or found the special weakness of each of its tenants and slowly drove them crazy with their inability to fight their instincts and base desires.

13

Durrell had certainly been responsible for bringing Val and me together. When the London café owner had conjured up the idea to re-create a Brighten wine café on the banks of the Thames, Durrell had suggested a theme of the Brighton Circle, a group of writers, I among them, who frequented such a café in Brighton for our self-important witty-repartee gatherings. And he had suggested portraits of the Brighton Circle writers at play for the café's walls as well as the matching of the trendy oil portraitist, the young Lord Cramner, with these subjects. The idea had seemed as brilliant and alive as we fancied ourselves to be and we all acquiesced with toasting and good cheer.

Quickly attached to our scheme, Val had me sit last. As eccentric and willful as he was brilliant, Val had me pose on warm summer evenings at the country estate his father, busy in Parliament, hardly ever graced, while he swirled around the canvas in just low-slung baggy cargo pant shorts. He was beautiful and young and vibrant, almost androgynous in his human perfection, and I couldn't help being smitten by him.

When, at last, he was ready for me, he simply stripped off his shorts and leaned down and took my surprised lips in his, unzipping my pants, as I sat at that café table, my arm numb from raising the glass in stiff pose. Holding my cock that had been hard for endless settings of watching him glide around his canvas in the nearly altogether, he descended his pert little buttocks into my lap and languidly fucked himself on what he found throbbing there to our mutual satiation.

I don't know exactly when he had made his decision to mold with me, but when I first was permitted to see the progress of his work on my portrait, he was painting me in the left quadrant of the canvas, against a luminous but austere painted rock wall, with the explanation that he wanted all of the life drawn forward to those sitting in the café chairs and enjoying the wine and cheese and bread—and absorbed in each other, with no competition from the world looming in the background. When I was permitted to view the work after we had fucked, the café chair in the right quadrant was being occupied with another figure, the artist himself, albeit in early stage. The facial features of both figures on the canvas unmistakably were Val and me—

but the lower half of the painting remained simply a rough sketch of bodies to come.

There are few secrets in the art world on the relatively small island of England, and the increasingly torrid love affair between Val and me was not one of them. Neither was a secret kept of my continued occasional casual-pickup man sex or of the sizzling scandal raised when after a particularly vigorous and invigorating Cambridge rugby match I attended with a Cambridge student son of a duke, I got drunk and let the duke's son and most of his rugby mates take turns fucking me throughout the night in his college rooms. I had always melted for vigorous and multiple partners, and I didn't give this adventure a second thought—until Val did.

Val gave it a loud and pointed second thought. And when Val's father heard the full extent of the unkept secrets, he also gave the matter a second thought. He gave Val an ultimatum. And Val, in turn, gave me an ultimatum: him or wantonness, not both. Val's father's ultimatum had been more stringent; it had excluded me from Val's life altogether.

Lawrence Durrell offered us a retreat at the villa he let for his writing escapes on the northern coast of Cyprus where we could escape together, wounded father unwitting. And I made my pledge to Val, telling him I chose him—and constancy—without reservation; that I could cut myself off from the siren song of casual lays and multiple partners if he would only have me still.

I didn't take this village and this house and its whisperings and enticements into account, though.

We'd been here for two months and still Val had not finished the portrait—or even gone in farther in painting himself back into the frame. He still wasn't sure of me. And he had every right not to be sure of me. I sat down repeatedly to work on my novel of the moment, and my hand repeatedly turned to the enticement of the smirking men of the café in the Bellapais square.

I had gone there once, quite innocently. But I had found myself ogling those laughing, muscular, hirsute Turkish men, with their easy, open enjoyment of life and their jovial camaraderie, their dusky skin and flashing eyes and curly black hair. And I found they were ogling me back. Sizing me up. Knowing that interesting and rich British men lodged at the Durrell villa. Thinking of what they could extract from me. Their slitted eyes telling me that sex was among the treasures they wondered might be attainable. I dared not let them see Val, so I avoided taking him there.

I did not go down to the square again. At least not until Val was asked to go into Nicosia for a weekend and speak on his art at a British Council program. If he only hadn't left me alone for that weekend.

Friday night I was restless and alone. An infrequent rain kept me trapped inside, and I picked up pen to work on a new chapter of my novel. I put pen to paper in the dim, flickering light of the desk lamp.

Ahh, the days of drifting down to the Tree of Idleness in the square in the late afternoon and sitting ogling the local Turkish Cypriot men and letting them ogle me until I got that certain look from one I fancied. Then taking him up . . .

I threw the pen down and cried out in my frustration. The electricity flicked and chose that moment to go out, no doubt in reaction to what passed as a rain storm on this arid island. I withdrew to the bedroom and lit the fire. I undid my sash and let my robe sink to the floor. The images pressed into my consciousness, starting my juices to flow. If Val were here, we'd be fucking. I closed my eyes and gave in to my furies.

And then back down to the square in the twilight after dinner with those fairy lights in the olive trees around the fringe of the stone café terrace, and, in that soft light and twittering laughter of the Mediterranean men and wisps of strong Turkish tobacco drifting up, eyeing and being eyed until I got the certain look from one I fancied and took him back up to the villa and let him fuck me in long, slow, sweeping strokes on the terrace under the stars.

My hands glided all up and down my body. I could hear the sound of the surf below above the pattering of the rain against the windows. I was stroking myself off, my eyes tightly shut, my body swaying back and forth on the balls of my feet in the heat coming off the flickering fireplace. I staggered and fell back on the bed and continued to stroke myself to completion, trying my best to bring the face and willowy body of my young lover into my imagination, but only seeing a swirl of grinning, dusky-skinned Turkish men down in the Bellapais square café clicking their tongues and making rude noises and gestures and grinning their knowing grins at me.

The next morning it was as if it hadn't rained for months. The sky was clear, the sun was hot, and the lap pool on the terrace was inviting. I dove in and swam laps, pulling myself along as quickly as I could, until I was near to exhaustion. I pulled myself out of the pool and padded over to the chaise lounge and collapsed, to sleep and dream.

And maybe, if he was really, really beautiful and masterful, taking him back to my bed for a night of sleep broken by brief periods of wanton lust, waking to the feel of a hot poker at my hole and a wheedling whisper for permission at my ear and arching back to accept the homage of a throbbing need to be deep inside me.

I opened my eyes to find that I had pushed my bathing trunks down and was stroking myself. Dusk was approaching, and the villa was whispering to me. Or was that the wind filtering through the pine trees higher up on the slopes of the Kyrenia Range mountains? And the surf. I could hear the surf. And the masculine, sing song voices of the Turkish men rising up from the Tree of Idleness café down the slope in the Bellapais square.

I rose up from the chaise lounge, like a zombie, stripped off my bathing trunks, and went through the French doors into the bedroom. I pulled on a pair of baggy cargo pant shorts and a mesh athletic T and a pair of sandals and moved toward the front door. I made a short detour into the studio. All this time and the painting wasn't finished. He still didn't trust me. We could not be complete, safe until he did. I could not be strong; as long as he questioned me, I could not trust myself. I was so weak.

I drifted down the narrow cobble-stone street, drawn by the light laughter and joking of the many-toned masculine voices. I sat at a café table beside a trellis supporting a rampant-bloomed climbing rose vine, just like the vibrant backdrop against which Val had painted me in England but had denied me on the canvas, and ordered a bottle of Cankaya wine. There was a brief silence across the square when I moved to the table, and then the chatter resumed. They seemed to be talking about me, though. They were ogling me and I ogled them.

It wasn't long before one of the younger, more handsome, more adventuresome of the Turkish men drifted over to my table and sat down and wondered if I might share my wine with him. That was fine with me. His smile was beautifully infectious. Once seated, though, he didn't want wine; he wanted Efes beer. This was fine with me; more wine for me. In time, two of us friends, also very presentable and good-humored, joined us and were more than pleased and convivial and attentive when I ordered more beer—and wine.

Later that night, the four of us stumbled up to the Bellapais villa. The first of the young men who had come to my table fucked me on the iron bed, me on my back with my legs spread and him standing between my legs and commanding my full attention with his flashing, laughing eyes as he enjoyed me in long languid strokes, while one of the other men got the fire going. When the first of the Turks was finished, he turned me on my belly, and the stouter, thicker-cocked of his two friends knelt at my head with his knees wedged below my chest and face fucked me while the third, profusely hirsute and muscular young man thrust hard and long and noisily inside me from the rear. The two exchanged places and the stouter of the Turks stretched me to the limit with his throbbing cock.

We all took a midnight swim in the lap pool on the terrace then, and they each fucked me again on the chaise lounge before prompting me to empty my billfold for them and stumbling jovially and satisfied back down the cobble-stone street to the coffee shop in the square, where the men's evening was still in full swing.

* * * *

Three days later, after a bout of heavy drinking on my part and a very satisfying but ultimately bitter sweet fucking of Val in our iron bed in front of a roaring fire, I awoke to an empty house. I called his name from the bed, wanting him again before we started our day. But there was nothing but silence. A strange silence. I heard no crashing of the Mediterranean surf, no masculine babbling from the square below. No whispering from the house. The house had won; it need not whisper enticingly to me again.

I knew he was gone before I rose from the bed. I pulled out bureau drawers and opened the closet, only to see what belonged to me, nothing that belonged to Val. I took up my robe and wrapped it around my shoulders and tied off the sash. I padded out to the study. There, on the top of the desk was the damning document. I looked down at the top sheet, and saw my own handwriting.

And then back down to the square in the twilight after dinner with those fairy lights in the olive trees around the fringe of the stone café terrace, and, in that soft light and twittering laughter of the Mediterranean men and wisps of strong Turkish tobacco drifting up, eyeing and being eyed until I got the certain look from one I fancied and took him back up to the villa and let him fuck me in long, slow, sweeping strokes on the terrace under the stars.

I was sure I had not left that out on the desk for Val to see.

I moved into the studio area of the room, hoping that I was wrong, that I would find him there, happily painting on our portrait. But, of course I wasn't wrong. The only evidence of Val still there was the painting. I went and stood in front of it. It took me several moments to really see it, to realize what he had done to it. The painting was finished now, but it no longer was a painting of Val and me at the table, saluting each other with raised glasses of wine. Where his figure had been was now, once again, a starkly sun-drenched ochre-painted stone wall fronted by an empty café chair. Val had evaporated. I knew then that Val irrevocably was lost to me. I sat alone at the table in the painting now. Had I really looked so sad in that painting all along?

I went back to the bedroom and sank onto the iron bed and cried myself to sleep. When I awoke, it was dusk. I rose, pulled on a pair of shorts, a T, and a pair of sandals, and gingerly made my way down the narrow cobble-stone road to the café in the Bellapais square. I picked out a table beside the trellis holding up the cascading vine of roses as darkness descended and the fairy lights in the olive trees around the fringe of the stone café terrace began to twinkle. And, in that soft light and twittering laughter of the Mediterranean men and wisps of strong Turkish tobacco drifting up, I eyed the men and I was eyed in return until I got the certain look from one I fancied. I spoke briefly with him and his equally hunky friend and took them back up to the villa and let them fuck me, in succession and then together, in long, slow, sweeping strokes on the terrace under the stars.

For the remainder of my time on the island, I frantically searched out the best artist I could find in Kyrenia, and when I found one, I had him paint me out of the painting as well—I could not bear being there alone—so that all that was left were two empty chairs and a table in front of an ochre-colored, sun-drenched stone wall.

I left the painting in the villa, hung over the desk where my damning thoughts had been confined to paper and discovered by my lost lover. Temporarily lost, I hoped. I knew I would be drawn back to the Bellapais villa—and I hoped that Val would be returning with me. And when he did, he would restore the two of us to that painting. Regardless of my urgings, I knew it was the two of us, together, eternally, who were meant to be in that painting and that it would have to remain devoid of humanity until we both were there.

Chapter 2: Kent Possession

by sabb

I had come there to my small rented villa in Bellapais for rest and inspiration and to escape from the crowded fast-paced life of America. As a writer myself, I had been enchanted by the romance of taking the British writer Lawrence Durrell's villa for six months, interested in seeing what inspiration it might hold for me, after I had found a unique and magical voice in the novels that formed his *Alexandria Quartet*—books he had written while living in the villa twenty years before. And I had soon been captivated by the island's rough bareness and the moods of the sea, by the old houses and the yachts moored in the small harbors. And by the men. Always at the villa my days had been filled by the men.

The villa itself seemed to raise my heat and urge me to go down to the café of the Tree of Idleness and return with company.

Ahh, the days of drifting down to the square after lunch and sitting around ogling the local Turkish Cypriot men and letting them ogle me. Until I got that certain look and took him up to my small rented villa and let him vigorously and noisily fuck my brains out on a lounger under the sun on the terrace overlooking the Mediterranean.

The villa itself always seemed to hum in the afterglow, as if it was pleased to be filled by the sights and sounds of sex, whether by day or night.

Or down to the square in the twilight after dinner, with those fairy lights in the olive trees around the fringe of the café's stone terrace. And, in that soft light, hearing the twittering laughter of the Mediterranean men and watching the wisps of strong Turkish tobacco smoke drifting up, as I was eyeing and being eyed. Until I got that certain look, and took him back up to the villa and let him fuck me in long, slow, sweeping strokes on the terrace under the stars.

While I lived in the villa I wanted more and more of what I found available under the Tree of Idleness in the village square, and I wanted it wilder and rougher. I was infatuated by what I had found, and I felt the villa tugging at me and urging me on to ever more abandoned behavior.

And maybe, if he was really, really beautiful and masterful, taking him back to my bed for a night of sleep broken up with brief periods of wanton lust, waking to the feel of a hot poker at my hole and a wheedling whisper for permission at my ear. Sighing "yes" and arching back to accept the homage of his throbbing need to be deep inside me. Breakfasting on the terrace by the small pool. Then pulling him into the pool and wrapping my legs around his waist, and letting the swirling water soften the rhythmic in and outing as I threw my head back and watched the morning Mediterranean light filter through the sighing branches of the olive trees. Thinking then about my after-lunch visit to the café on the square, already assessing which eyes I would respond to that day.

But then there was a day when there had been few men about at the café when I went there, and the rough handling I'd had from half a dozen men the night before had left me wanting something different. So that for a change a beautiful young man's big dark bedroom eyes and demure long lashes had caught my attention and my thoughts.

He was staring at me from several tables away, his eyes filled with longing in a serious brooding way, and somehow that afternoon it had been him I had taken back up the hill to my villa. And he was carrying a bag I hadn't noticed had been sitting under his table. Halfway up the path I can remember being uncertain and fleetingly regretting my choice. But I knew I could go back to the café that evening and find another man more to my taste. Bigger, stronger, rougher. The brooding young man accompanying me was only for the afternoon.

At the villa, it was I who fucked his brains out, as he surrendered to me, lying back and lifting and opening his legs wide. His big eyes closing and the long lashes fluttering against his cheeks as he threw his head back when I entered him. His cries and whimpers at my rough taking of him satisfying my need to possess forcefully for a change.

But when he was naked, I had found that his lithe olive-skinned body was surprisingly strong and muscular and flexible, his arms strong, his fingers long and slender and alive. And his cock was large. Large and thick. But it was my turn to fuck someone. He was still there in the evening when I was finally exhausted and fell into a fitful sleep, wondering if I should tell him to go.

Like most of the men I brought home, he spoke English with a broken local accent and I gave little thought to who he was. But he knew who I was, and seemed impressed that I could write well, though I was hardly famous then. I had only had one book published, in my native America. Not what I would have expected a young man living in Turkish Cyprus to have read, and it amused me, but I gave it no more thought.

I awoke early the next morning to find him sitting on the bed, gazing at me broodingly with his bag in his lap. Then his eyes dropped to the bag and he pulled out a worn copy of my book and his fingers moved to open the pages and he read passages from it in his quaint accented English, and told me how wonderful he thought it was.

I took the book from him, flattered at his admiration, and he looked up at me then with a small smile on his lips and complete concentration on his face, and it was a look that also connected me to him. Then his eyes dropped to watch my hands as I signed my name and wrote a short dedication in the front. "To Lawrence, with thanks and fond memories."

"I am named after the first great writer who lived here, many years ago. After Lawrence Durrell," he said shyly.

When I gave the book back, he placed it carefully in his bag, and I ran my hand up his inner thigh and between his spread legs and began to stroke his partly full, long, thick cock. It was a tool that had surprised me on such a lean, young man, a rod I would have wanted to feel making its way into my ass if I had thought he wanted to take and possess me. And would do it roughly.

But I was the one doing the possessing with him, and as I stroked him up, I moved my mouth to his and pushed him back on the bed. He lifted his legs for me again, and when I ended the kiss, I began tonguing at his hole, which quickly loosened to my attention. Then I was holding my cock and pressing the head to his entrance and beginning another journey inside his passage. He arched back, surrendering to me again, and I reached out and stroked a hand through the trail of hair running up his belly to his pecs and pinched his nipples, making him gasp and reach for me, to pull me closer to him. But I stayed back, watching him stroking his own tool as he felt my length stuffing him deep.

His beautiful cock spouted cum, and I came myself at the sight of it, before leaning in and licking the cream from his belly and chest. Then with a deep sigh, I slipped out of him and went to shower and dress.

After that, I was hungry and needed food, and we left the villa together, with him carrying the bag he had so carefully returned my book to. He shook my hand seriously as we parted where the laneway joined a wider lane just before we reached the village square, and he shyly reminded me that his name was Lawrence. Then he turned along the path that ran to the back of the village as I turned toward the café on the square among the olive trees, and I forgot him.

Inside Sami Ergun's café, the Tree of Idleness, the atmosphere was the same as always, but different in some way, and I was ogled by a dark young man with rough strong hands, who I found when I took him home, was very forceful and full of stamina, so that I moaned and cried out how he was taking me as I had never been taken before.

Then I had to finish some research in Turkey and left on the Monday, flying to Istanbul. But a couple of weeks later I was back at the villa. On that first night, I walked down to the café in the soft warm air of the evening, coming upon the wonderful sight of the fairy lights in the old olive trees and welcomed by the whisper of men's voices and their quiet laughter.

The place was busy, and I settled onto a stool to ogle the men and wait for that look from one I wanted to look at me. But almost at once someone started playing the baglama, the favorite instrument of traditional Turkish musicians, and there was a man singing and I looked over and saw that it was him, my recent lover, Lawrence, sitting to one side of the baglama player on a chair, his look brooding and intense as he sang the words to some traditional melody.

The baglama player was lost in the beauty of his music. I had learned his name was Kemal, and I had tried to attract his attention for weeks. He was one of the most handsome of the young men who came to the square. But he only had attention for his music—and for the young student who sat beside him, playing the second baglama. That was Basir, I knew, the son of my Landlady, Layla Ergun, Lawrence Durrell's old friend. I had met the boy, shy but winsome, down at Layla's house in the harbor town of Kyrenia when I had picked up the key to the villa.

Lawrence, the singer, looked up at some point and saw me, and for a moment a connection flared briefly between us, and after that his eyes frequently fixed intensely on me. All the other men's eyes were on the three achingly beautiful young men as they played and sang, and I felt oddly alone as the men who usually ogled me admired them instead. But it was the music, I told myself, that made them watch the trio.

Then a beautiful man who had made forceful love to me before was giving me that look, and he rose and left the café and I met him in the dark on the cobbled lane, and we made our way together up to my villa.

He was as rough with me as he had been before, and after he had taken me on the lounger on the terrace, we went inside to the bedroom, where he pushed me back on the bed and, holding my hands high above my head, fucked down into me, his cock circling and pumping shallowly, and I was moaning and had closed my eyes, moving my hips in time with his, lost in heat. But then he stopped moving, and I felt his weight shift. I looked up and saw him backing off, pulling out of me.

"Hey, No, no. Don't stop," I cried huskily, reaching for him in confusion and then seeing someone behind him.

It was Lawrence, looking wild and angry and pulling my partner back. Pulling him away as I tried to pull him back to me.

"Hey, what's going on?" I shouted, confused.

And even in the aroused state I was in, the change in the look of Lawrence's dark eyes was obvious and made me frightened.

In a moment my companion was free and pulling on his clothes in a rush. But Lawrence was gripping my ankles and jerked my body roughly down the bed. I tried to grab hold of something to stop being pulled to the floor, but Lawrence was surprisingly strong, and his big dark eyes were blazing black with fury. And I couldn't get a grip on anything but the sheets.

"What are you doing?" I yelped.

"You, you American writer, you . . . ," he hissed at me.

My earlier companion was hurrying out of the door as my feet hit the floor hard, and Lawrence gripped my upper arms tightly, his long lean fingers biting into them like steel hooks.

I was now as much frightened as confused and aimed a kick at him that landed badly. In reply, he gave my face the back of his free hand, and I cried out in shock, feeling the pain of a small cut in my lip and briefly tasting blood.

"I am a real man," he hissed, "Do you think I would have let you take me like, like that, if I had known what you really are?"

It took me a moment to understand what he was saying. "You didn't have to do anything, I didn't force you," I replied in confused helplessness.

I understood what it meant to be a real man in Turkish Cyprus, that it was acceptable to fuck and be sucked off by another man, but not considered manly to be the one taken. But I was totally confused, because Lawrence had given himself to me so willingly.

He was dragging me out of the bedroom, and I struggled to pull free. To kick him, to do anything to stop whatever was going on. He was no longer the lean and gentle young man I had fucked the previous weekend. Now his eyes were black ice and cold, his mouth thin and cruel. And I was shocked to find he was far too strong for me.

Lawrence dragged me through the doorway into the courtyard of my villa, where he held me by the upper arm as he pulled the wrought iron gate that I never used, closed over the entrance to the house. It banged into place with a heavy clang. Then he pushed me back against it, hard.

Anyone high up on the adjoining roofs and houses could see us there. Me naked and looking out, Lawrence still dressed and hunched over, holding me there, one long, elegant hand grasping both my wrists together painfully as he reached for something. He changed hands briefly, then he had his shirt off and pushed my wrists high up, stretching me, using his extra height and power.

He pressed his body hard against mine, pinning me back against the hard steel of the gate while using his shirt to tie my wrists to the fancy iron. I was frightened and I realized that if he really hurt me, there was no one nearby who'd know that my screams were not the usual ones of me being well fucked.

"What are you doing?" I croaked.

He said nothing, his eyes black with anger and the knots at my wrists being tied tight. The cotton shirt jerked so that it felt like a steel band.

His body, pressed against me, was giving me familiar messages, though. His prick was a hard rod pressed against my lower belly and against my own hard tool. The rough manhandling and his strength and domination turning me on in spite of my growing fear. Or perhaps the fear also turning me on.

Now I was babbling, asking him why, begging him not to do this. Telling him anything I could think of to calm him. My heart thumping wildly.

When he had me secured, he stepped back and dropped his pants and kicked them off, and his briefs followed. Then he grabbed both my legs, lifting them up so all my weight suddenly hung from my tied wrists. I cried out, but he just pushed my knees back to my chest and parted them.

"Oh god," I whimpered. "No, no." Suddenly wanting what I knew was coming, but afraid of what he might be capable of.

Then he was at my hole and he held one of my legs up with his shoulder as his fingers began to show me how far they could reach inside me, long and flexible, probing and exploring. One long one sinking deep, then two starting to stretch me and putting pressure where it had the most effect, me starting to leak juice from my cock and jerking and moaning for more. Whimpering as Lawrence added a third finger to his explorations.

I came when he added a fourth finger and had me so stretched that I was yelping that I couldn't take it any more. And I was sure I couldn't.

"I can't. I can't take it," I cried.

Then he gripped his cock and forced himself into me roughly, but, yes, just the way I liked it. My arms felt stretched beyond endurance as he entered me, but his pumping hips lifted my butt with each thrust he made into me, taking me like a wild animal in heat.

His long lashes were hooding his black eyes as he gazed down, watching his big thick phallus moving wildly in and out of my ass. His balls slapping my butt. I moaned and rolled my hips. I wanted this. Wanted it in spite of his long fingers biting into my calves as he held them high. In spite of the pain in my stretched arms.

As he plowed me, the skin on my back was being rubbed raw against the rusty wrought iron of the old gate, but I didn't feel it. And soon I was yelping, begging him for more and ejaculating for a second time, up our bellies, my cream mingling in his trail of hair. A moment later he bottomed hard inside me, and I felt him spasm and cum, again and again, filling me.

And I moaned, "Yes. Yes. Fuck me. Don't stop. Never stop."

When he was done, he withdrew from me, and as his cum trickled down my inner thigh, he opened the gate, leaving me hanging, stretched out on the pattern of wrought iron, as he moved behind me. My legs hung down now with my toes barely on the ground as he parted my cheeks and gripped my hips, and his strong hands reached through the wrought iron gate and entered me again, already hard enough to do it. Young and virile, and in a mindless heat.

I lifted my legs, trying to ease his entry, trying to rest my feet in the curves of the iron behind me. One foot found a support, and some of the strain went from my arms. Lawrence now fucked me hard from behind, the tightness giving me a feeling of being plowed by a baseball bat. He gripped my hips and swung my body roughly back and forth as he fucked me. My own cock quickly hard again and slapping against my belly.

Then, looking across the courtyard, I saw two small boys standing wide eyed on the open roof of an adjoining house.

"Lawrence," I said. "Kids," I was hardly able to think, "on the roof."

He took a few moments to register what I was saying. Then he yelled at them and they fled, and he pumped me faster, before stopping, pulling me back onto the steel gate, and filling me again. Then he pulled out of me with a plop and a release of cum that made me groan loudly, and he went and closed the heavy double doors into the courtyard. Doors that had been carved a century before from heavy timber towed as a tree trunk behind a boat, all the way from Anatolia. Long before the villa had been let by an English writer named Lawrence Durrell, my rough young lover's namesake.

He came back to me and halted in front of me, looking half angry still, but embarrassed too. The tension and fear drained out of me, and I moaned with pain, suddenly feeling my arms aching and also the grazes on my back from the rusted wrought iron burning painfully.

"I was in awe of you. I would have done anything to be with you," he said, which made no sense. "But I am a man," he added proudly.

"I noticed," I said, smiling weakly, completely spent and satiated.

"One day soon I will marry, have children, take my proper place. But . . . your writing," he said, "It is so moving."

When he had released me, we fell into bed, and he made strong but gentle love to me, and I felt the villa humming, perhaps more than ever before.

"I have to go to Nicosia for a couple of days," Lawrence told me in the morning, "but then I will be back and visit you again. On Sunday night." He said it as if there was no discussion and there wasn't. I wanted him to visit me again. To make the villa hum loudly again.

When he was gone I dozed and later stroked myself, aroused just by the thought of him returning. But later that afternoon I was visited by my landlady, Layla.

My lease had been for six months, and I had asked a month before if I could extend it. Layla had frowned. "I am not sure, Mr. Kent. I may have an old friend, Mark Amalfi, who said he may be coming to the villa again, but he has not yet sent me a deposit," she said.

I had heard nothing from her since and having been away had conveniently forgotten this might be my last few days at the villa. And now Layla Ergun was at my door, saying, "I am sorry, Mr. Kent. You were not here the last two weeks, and I myself had to go to my father's village for a few days, so I could not tell you sooner. I am sorry. But no. You will have to go tomorrow. The other man, Mark, is an old friend who has stayed here before. A nice man like you. Like all my favorite tenants. But one I have known longer, who is ill and longs to return here, perhaps one last time."

I understood there was more than a simple lease involved and knew my time was up. I wanted to know how I could get in touch with Lawrence, but almost couldn't bring myself to ask.

"Lawrence?" Layla laughed, "That is not a Turkish name. There has only been one Lawrence here. Lawrence Durrell, the famous writer. I know of no young man in Bellapais called Lawrence."

When I drove my car filled with my few possessions to the airport on Friday afternoon, I doubted I would ever return or ever see Lawrence again. And I was hit by a wave of loss, for Lawrence and for the villa and my wildly promiscuous life there. But mostly for him, for Lawrence. More than I would have believed. And I wondered who he was.

I decided to spend a few weeks in Istanbul before returning to the states and two weeks after leaving Turkish

Cyprus I was at a friend's house there for dinner, and I suddenly felt dizzy, and instead of waiting for the maid to bring me water, I made my own way to the kitchen to get some. There was a TV up on top of the refrigerator tuned to the local TV station, and as I passed it, I glanced up, and was even dizzier. He was there. Lawrence. In a suit and tie. I hardly recognized him. He was sitting stiffly in a chair on a small stage, his dark eyes magnetic, he mouth moving more than I had ever seen it move before, as he spoke in a language I couldn't understand properly. The other chair was occupied by the smooth, aging Turk who was hosting the program, Tayyip Babacan, who was interviewing Lawrence. I grabbed the maid by the arm and pulled her over, not taking my eyes from the small screen.

"Who is he, who is he? The young man in the chair on the TV?" I demanded.

She turned up the sound and watched for a few minutes. "Someone from Turkish Cyprus, he is talking about old folk songs. He sings and plays the baglama too," she added, pleased at that.

"His name?" I asked.

"Mustafa."

"What is his family name?" I asked her, frustrated.

She shrugged, "They are not saying."

Then she twisted free of my grip, and I stood mesmerized, watching him. Knowing how his hands felt on, and inside me, wanting to feel them again and feel him filling me and mining me, for the sounds I made, telling him how good it was. Or to just have him watching me with those huge bedroom eyes of his, with their long deceptively demure lashes, as I stroked myself and he read words to me.

But the maid had turned to continue with her work.

"I need to know," I said, and she half-heartedly tried to watch the TV and lay small pieces of baklava on a large plate at the same time.

Mustafa moved off the small stage and to one side, where two young women stood and a man holding a baglama sat waiting. Then he took his place beside the man, sitting down and taking up his baglama and beginning to play. The women were now smiling and joined in, singing some popular folk song. Both

31

women were beautiful in the dark Turkish way, and I felt my heart sink as I wondered if one of them was soon to be his wife. Or if the man, who was rather gaunt and ugly, was being fucked by him.

I had rarely had bouts of jealousy, and I was surprised by my reaction.

When the song was over, the host of the program appeared with the group to thank them, and gave their names to the audience.

"Mustafa, Mustafa Ergun." I caught it.

"Mustafa Ergun," the maid said without looking up, "That is his name. They say he's from Cyprus. They say he's been playing there for a long time, for twenty years or more?"

"Twenty years," I muttered. "That can't be. Surely he's only about twenty years old."

The maid looked up at the television and gave a low laugh. "More like thirty years," she said. And then she laughed and muttered something about foreigners and guessing the ages of Turkish people.

I barely had time to let that sink in when the last name hit me. Ergun. Layla's married name was Ergun. And the last name of Sami at the Tree of Idleness café also was Ergun. He must be related to them, I realized, with a shock—which perhaps explained everything. Perhaps there was no old friend returning to the villa. Perhaps the shame of "Lawrence's" taking wasn't a village secret.

Then the maid hurried from the kitchen, carrying a large tray laden with small coffee cups and the plate of baklava. And the program ended, and I filled a glass with bottled water and downed it before returning to the living room.

"I have to go," I said to my host and his wife.

I explained, apologizing and saying I was still not feeling right. A taxi was called, and I gave my address. But once the cab door was closed and we had moved off, I leant forward to the driver and changed our destination.

The taxi double-parked in the busy street, and I looked across at the front of the television station building. It had taken over thirty minutes to get there, and I was sure he would have left already, but I paid off the taxi and sprinted across the four lanes of traffic to the footpath on the other side, outside the building. And then I hesitated and paced around before I walked in and asked if Mustafa Ergun had left yet, hoping it hadn't been a prerecorded show. Tayyip Babacan's show was supposed to be live, but I never believed everything I saw on TV.

The man on the reception desk had little English and didn't understand me, so I had to leave and stand outside the building. Waiting. Sure Mustafa and the others must have left the studio already but unable to go until I was certain I had missed him.

Two hours later I finally gave up waiting and caught a taxi to a bar I knew, where I was able to forget.

Chapter 3: Secret Possession

by sabb

When Baris was still a child, he had been pushed up next to me to join in when I was playing at cafés near Kyrenia. He was only a child of ten when I first met him, and his mother, Layla, the sister-in-law of the owner of a café in Bellapais I often played my baglama at, the Tree of Idleness, was keen for him to learn from me. But I was already too busy settling into life as a husband and father and was not interested in regularly teaching a child so young, though Layla pushed me hard and I grudgingly gave her son some guidance.

For a while he seemed to fall from sight, but then Layla had brought him to me again when he was fifteen. The same age I had been when my parents were killed in a car crash in Turkey. I knew that, like me, he was a foreigner, not a true Turkish Cypriot by blood, and that, like me again, he would never be truly accepted as one of them.

And he had talent. From that time when I met him as a young man, I had wanted him to succeed, to escape the island and become someone, become himself. Unlike me. I could have escaped, gone to England and made another life, but when I was eighteen, it had seemed too hard, so I had given in and tried to belong, even though I knew I never would. Part of me was joined to the island by my mother's blood, and now that I was married, with children, I knew I would never leave it more than briefly.

But Baris. Baris I wanted to fly free. So, finally I took him as a student as his mother always wanted.

"He wants to play like that pop star, Kemal. Play the guitar, not just the baglama. But not electric." She had said, "But I want him to play the baglama; it will be good if he plays that well. Always at the cafés they want a baglama player. There he will meet many people."

It was only later that I understood why she wanted him to meet many people.

So I had taken him as a student. My only student, because I held a high position in the Turkish civil service and had no need to take on students. And if I wanted to play and encourage others, I did it in the cafés, in friend's homes, and occasionally at concerts organized by various cultural organizations. The cultural attaché at the Canadian high commission at that time was very interested in traditional Turkish music.

For three years I taught Baris and watched him grow into a beautiful young man. Each year my feelings for him grew, but I did nothing about them. But each year on his birthday I ached for him to pass into manhood. And also I dreaded that day.

I had made my accommodations with life. I had married, I had given up the chance I'd had to escape, and now I was bound by the social rules that governed a man's life in Turkish Cyprus.

But Baris. One day Baris was suddenly eighteen years old and I was invited to Layla's house for the celebrations. I was too full of emotions to have my wife accompany me and made some excuse of probably staying over rather than driving home drunk. She frowned on my drinking any alcohol. She made a disapproving sound and said no more. We get on well enough, but there is no great love between us.

Many relatives had come to the celebrations, and Layla's house was full. And Baris took me aside when I arrived and told me that if I wished to stay the night, the old villa nearby in Bellapais was empty. He looked at me with his big eyes as he told me this. Beautiful eyes.

I said, "Thank your mother for me, Baris. As you know, I don't like to drive after drinking. That's how my parents died."

He knew the story of how their small car had been hit by a drunken truck driver on a dark road near Bursa while returning from the cemeteries at Gallipoli, which my father had been inspecting in his work with the Commonwealth War graves commission.

All night I was nervous, hardly able to tear my eyes from Baris, my body aching with longing for him. And of course we played the baglama together. I had brought my instrument with me, and half way through the evening two chairs were organized in the courtyard under a light, and we took our places. Baris's repertoire was large already, and he had grown to have a true appreciation for the traditional melodies and songs of the island, as a stranger often does, and had a fine voice also, far better than mine. So we played and sang together, and, playing together, we were able to look into each other's eyes, to smile and share an intimate connection in public without it seeming wrong. Several times that night I was glad the baglama hid what my tented pants would have clearly shown I felt as we played together.

The party went on late, and all I wanted was for it to end and for Baris to guide me up to this villa he had said I could sleep in, and for us to have a few moments alone. I have no idea what I expected that night. I longed only for even a moment alone with him. I was sure he had similar feelings for me. I was sure. But I was equally afraid I might be wrong. I had made no move. I had tried to make the growing feelings stop, to be just a good teacher to him. But sometimes we cannot stop ourselves from falling in love, however wrong and dangerous we know it is.

Then Baris was beside me again. "I am tired," he said, yawning. "Do you want me to show you to the villa? Or would you—?"

"No, you show me now. I am tired too," I said, shaking my head as if it was full of sleep. "A busy day and a very good party."

I said good night to Layla. "And how will you get back, Baris?" she asked distractedly.

He shrugged, "If I can't get back tonight, I will stay at the villa also, and Kemal can drive me down in the morning," he replied. "Don't worry. I am a man now."

And then Layla hugged him, "A man, a man," she said, echoing his words back to him, and then she waved us away.

I was almost shaking as I drove the winding road up the hillside, Baris silent beside me apart from giving directions.

"This is the famous Durrell villa," Baris suddenly said, as the car climbed the cobbled lane. "The famous English writer. I am named for him. Baris Lawrence Ergun," he said proudly as I stopped the car by the villa's entrance.

"Well Baris Lawrence Ergun, that is a fine name for a very fine young man."

We sat there in silence for a minute, both apparently not sure what to do, until I opened the car door. "Well, we can't sit out here all night." I said.

"Sorry," Baris apologized, suddenly hurrying out of the car and rummaging in his pockets for the big old key that opened the doors while I took my overnight bag from the trunk of the car.

I followed him inside as he turned on the lights and led the way in. "The bathroom," he said, indicating a room built off the entrance foyer, "and the bedroom," he said indicating the door at the far side of the entrance. "Living room, kitchen," he added unnecessarily, waving a hand to the side and then hurrying through and opening French doors from the living room onto a terrace. "And the terrace."

He walked back into the living room and over to a small bookcase where he removed a worn book and opened it and walked back to me. "There have been other writers who have lived here since Lawrence Durrell. Have you heard of Mark Amalfi?" he asked me nervously, handing me the book.

"No," I replied, sure I had not and aching for Baris and wondering where this was leading as I looked down and opened the book where it naturally fell open.

Someone had underlined several paragraphs, and the words leapt out at me from the page.

Ahh, the days of drifting down to the Tree of Idleness in the square in the late afternoon and sitting ogling the local Turkish Cypriot men and letting them ogle me until I got that certain look from one I fancied. Then taking him up to my rented villa and letting him vigorously, joyously, and noisily fuck my brains out on a lounger under the sun on the terrace overlooking the Mediterranean.

Or down to the square in the twilight after dinner, with those fairy lights in the olive trees around the fringe of the café's stone terrace. And, in that soft light hearing the twittering laughter of the Mediterranean men and watching the wisps of strong Turkish tobacco smoke drifting up, as I was eyeing and being eyed. Until I got that certain look and took him back up to the villa and let him fuck me in long, slow, sweeping strokes on the terrace under the stars.

And then back down to the square in the twilight after dinner with those fairy lights in the olive trees around the fringe of the stone café terrace, and, in that soft light and twittering laughter of the Mediterranean men and wisps of strong Turkish tobacco drifting up, eyeing and being eyed until I got the certain look from one I fancied and took him back up to the villa and let him fuck me in long, slow, sweeping strokes on the terrace under the stars.

And maybe, if he was really, really beautiful and masterful, taking him back to my bed for a night of sleep broken by brief periods of wanton lust, waking to the feel of a hot poker at my hole and a wheedling whisper for permission at my ear and arching back to accept the homage of a throbbing need to be deep inside me. Breakfasting on the terrace by the small pool and then pulling him into the pool and wrapping my legs around his waist and letting the swirling water soften the rhythmic in and outing as I threw my head back and watched the morning Mediterranean light filter through the sighing branches of the olive trees and thought about my late afternoon visit to the Tree of Idleness café in the Bellapais square, already assessing which eyes I would respond to today.

The underlining ended, and I looked up, stunned, and saw Baris walking through the French doors and out into the night, outside onto the dimly lit terrace. Reaching the far wall, he leaned back against it and looked at me.

That book told me that he knew something of what I might be. But what was in the book was nothing to do with me; it was a world I did not belong to. My world was here, now, looking out at Baris standing there looking at me.

Inviting. So inviting. The pale light of the full moon lit his head and body in a soft silver glow, and I caught my breath and almost fell he was so achingly beautiful. And I couldn't stop myself. I moved to him and embraced him and pulled him close.

39

"I want you," I whispered, "I want you, Baris."

Suddenly his arms were about me, and his face to mine and our lips were pressed together. A childish, innocent closed-mouth kiss.

"I love you, Kemal," he whispered back, and I could feel him shaking. "I've loved you since the first day. And now I am a man; now no one can stop us," he said, talking in a frenzy and pressing his hot hard manhood to my own throbbing pole.

I was tugging at his clothes, trying to free his body, reach his skin, rubbing my cock against his. Wanting. Wanting as I had never wanted before. Overwhelmed to know that he wanted me too. He pulled at my clothes too, my neat business shirt, tearing it at the buttons as his fingers failed to work. He was so ready, and I have no idea how, but I was sinking to my knees and taking his virgin young man's hard penis in my lips and kissing it, tasting the liquid that ran from the tiny slit in its cap. Making love to him as my hands encased and trembled at the full firmness of his sac and the soft skin of his round firm ass.

His fingers tangled in my hair, and he moaned and whimpered and began to rock his hips, moving his cock into me, deeper, deeper. And I opened my throat for him, wanting him at my core.

It was only moments before he came, filling me with his hot seed.

Now I ached to possess him. But I would not rush that first taking. No, that was to be savored as a gift of love.

Instead, we kissed. This time me parting his lips with my tongue and tasting his sweet breath for the first time. He was uncertain. At once allowing me in, then fighting to possess my mouth.

His hand reached my throbbing rod, and his fingers tentatively stroked and explored it, and I moaned loudly. "Ohhhhh, yes. Ohhhhhhhh. Baris. Baris." And like some inexperienced teenager myself, I shot my first load over his hand like that.

We lay against each other then, recovering. Both still firm and full of heat. Over his shoulder and off to the east below us I could see lights, the lights of the village square and the Tree of Idleness café, with the voices of men floating up to us on the

40

night air. It was only then that I realized the terrace wall was at the edge of a rocky cliff, and I was horrified to realize that pushing Baris back the way I was was dangerous, and I hurriedly pulled him in to me and away from the edge.

"There is a drop," I said, "I might have pushed you over," and I hugged him hard to me, knowing I had almost pushed him up on to the wall so I could part his legs and bury my face between the mounds of his ass.

"If I had fallen and died now, I would be happy," he replied, nuzzling my neck, "perfectly happy."

But not letting go of him, I led him into the house and on to the bedroom, leaving our clothes scattered on the terrace.

I lay him back on the old iron bed and covered his body in kisses. Naked, he obviously was not a true Turkish Cypriot, being not so heavy or dark enough or as hirsute. When I had covered every part of his front with my mouth, I turned him over and kissed his back and up and down his legs before I parted them and buried my face between those firm mounds of his ass and opened him. I wanted Baris to have a better life than I had had, to have a better future, to have no regrets and to never suffer for loving me, for surrendering his manhood to me.

And when I took him that first time, I knew I wanted him to possess me as fully.

I had to convince him. For I found he worshipped me, and he knew that a real man in Turkish Cyprus never gives himself to another; he only takes.

"I will never be a real Turkish Cypriot, Baris," I whispered to him as we lay together. "I will never be like the men who sip coffee in the café beneath the Tree of Idleness. And I want to have you reach the center of me, to feel you possess me, and if you fuck me, I shall truly feel you at my heart."

He was tentative, but he was also young and virile, and he rode me as well as any man could. And as no other man ever had, or has since. For he is the only one I can show my true self too.

We play the baglama together often at the cafés, and we meet when we can. But it is not so safe to be as we are, and there are not enough places or times when it is safe for us to be together. For men here cannot be real lovers and remain real men.

He is a fine musician, and I have written to a friend in Istanbul, who has contacts, to see if we can find Baris a place with a folk group there. Some travel to Europe regularly and I am sure that a good Turkish Cypriot musician could make a living in Germany.

His mother, Layla, wants it too. She has some idea what sort of man he is and hopes one of the well-off foreign tenants of the villa in Bellapais will take him away. But he is a man, and I hope he can make his own way. This is not the place for him.

Yes, one day Baris will leave here and be free.

Chapter 4: Henson Possession

by habu

I would have never known sheer ecstasy or just how wanton I naturally was if it hadn't been for the British diplomat and writer Lawrence Durrell. And it wasn't really because of his writing, either; it was because of his mountainside villa in the ancient Byzantine abbey town of Bellapais on the steep slopes of the Kyrenia Mountains in the Turkish zone of Cyprus.

I had become hooked on Durrell's writing when his *Alexandria Quartet* had been natural background reading for my stint as an economic affairs officer at the Canadian embassy in Cairo, Egypt. And then it had been a slam dunk that I would have read his classic about the Cyprus civil war period, *Bitter Lemons*, when I shortly was moved over to that Mediterranean island to head up the cultural affairs office there.

I had been in Cyprus' inland capital, Nicosia, for no longer than a week on my new assignment to the Canadian High Commission there and was still living in the Nicosia Hilton, when the local Greek Cypriot staff housing officer came to me all aglow at the great "find" they had made for my housing on the Turkish side of the border. We were barely six years removed from the 1974 Turkish invasion of Cyprus that had prompted the division of the island into two belligerent zones, and Canada was doing its best, both Greece and Turkey being among its key European allies, to balance its approach to an island with warring Greek and Turkish inhabitants and a hot

43

border. I had to conduct economic development programs on both sides of the island targeted at getting Cyprus in the European Community at last, and the border often was closed. So, I needed digs in both zones.

"Mr. Henson, Mr. Henson," the Greek Cypriot housing officer, Panos, said breathlessly as I left the high commissioner's morning meeting. "We've found the perfect place for you on the Turkish side. It's not in the Turkish zone of Nicosia, but I think it will please you. It's in a village above Kyrenia, which is on the Mediterranean coast and just a twenty-five minute drive from the Nicosia border checkpoint."

That seemed a bit far from the capital to me, and I was about to say something, when he continued.

"It's a villa that the British writer, Lawrence Durrell, let in the mountainside village of Bellapais while he was working in the British High Commission here. It's where he wrote that group of four books of his about Egypt.

"*The Alexandria Quartet*," I said.

"Yes, that one."

It was fate. I was hooked. I didn't know it then, but the villa had picked me out. It knew me. Better than I knew myself.

I knew even then, of course, that I preferred men. But I didn't know what that villa knew about me—that I preferred men frequently and in multiple couplings. And the remote village of Bellapais, in the Turkish zone, where few of the people I worked with in the Greek zone could even go, proved to be perfection for me and the appetites I so soon would learn that I had.

It started that first day I drove north from Nicosia, across the Kyrenia Mountain range pass, and down into the ancient castle harbor town of Kyrenia to take the keys of the Bellapais house from the landlady who had managed the property from the time of Durrell's occupancy. I was somewhat anxious to meet the woman. Layla wasn't either Greek or Turkish Cypriot. I understood she was Egyptian, and it had been hinted to me that she had been more than just a landlady to Durrell—and that, in fact, she may have been an inspiration for one of the primary characters in his *Quartet*.

"You are a writer, I can tell," Layla, the landlady, said to me as soon as she had finished pouring a glass of wine for me in the sunny courtyard of her Kyrenia house. I could not discern how old she was—she certainly wasn't young. But she was still a handsome woman and had a serenity about her that was very calming. And when she looked at me, I felt like she could reach into the very depths of my thinking. This feeling was so strong that I pulled my tweed jacket closely about me; there were things about me that I would not want a landlady to know.

"Yes, I guess I am a writer of sorts," I answered, not knowing why my admission caused her to smile so deeply for me. "I do dabble and have published a few things. I guess that's why the Durrell house attracts me."

"Yes, yes, I knew it would. The house has called to you. I can tell that."

How strange, I thought. She looked like a normal person, but what was this she was babbling about? A villa with a mind of its own? A villa that called out to its occupants and picked and chose who lived there? Well, if it had put me in the category of Lawrence Durrell, I supposed I should feel flattered.

"I understand the villa has been empty for some time," I said, wondering what that meant about it's condition and it's hidden failings.

"Yes," Layla answered. The smile briefly left her face. There have been tenants who have come and gone. The one here the longest after Lawrence was a nice Australian man—his name was Taylor. He was much like you, but Australian. The villa has been waiting for him, but he hasn't returned. I think it has grown tired of waiting, and that this is why you are here. Yes, I think this is just right."

"You say he left?"

"Yes, when the Turks came in 1974, he got scared along with all of the Greeks and the foreigners, and he went over the mountain and into Nicosia and I haven't seen him since." Layla gave a sigh and sat down in the chair across from me then. "If only I'd been able to tell him. He was safe. The Turks would not have harmed him. I would have seen to that, and Bellapais was declared off limits. It was known to be a foreigners' artist village.

The house has been so sad since then. He made the villa come alive, just as I know you will.

"Alister Taylor was a writer too, just like you and my dear Lawrence—and that writer who came and lived in the villa for nearly ten years before the fighting started here. Oh, so tragic, that one. Mark, Mark Amalfi. He and his artist friend seemed so happy together—at first. And then Mr. Taylor has difficulty writing in the villa too. He kept telling me it was haunted by dangerous . . . what did he call them? Urges, yes, urges. I thought that was strange."

I had been half listening to her rambling reminiscing, but a familiar name sliced through my own wandering contemplations of what I would have to do to get the services turned on in the villa—the high commission's Greek maintenance staff on the other side of the barricaded Green Line would be of no help to me here in the Turkish-held zone of the island. "Mark Amalfi? Was that the writer Mark Amalfi?"

"Yes, that's him," Layla said. You know him?

"No, not personally, but I believe he wrote a book about Cyprus too, didn't he? A novel of some controversy, if I remember correctly."

"Yes, he titled it *The Tree of Idleness* after the coffee house in the square at Bellapais," Layla said. "I believe I have a copy over here. Yes, yes, here's one. Would you like to borrow it to read up at the villa? I think there should be a copy there too, but you may borrow this one to be sure. He wrote it there, you know. Although I should not like to lose this copy. He sent it to me with a very nice inscription inside."

"Yes, yes, thanks," I answered. "I would like to read it again where he wrote it. I've brought copies of *The Alexandria Quartet* to do so as well."

I well remembered the controversy of that book. It got good reviews in the literary circles at the time, but it was written in a time when men having relationships with men was still quite scandalous. And the scandal of Amalfi taking up with the high-strung artist son of that English earl had brought back comparisons of the years of Oscar Wilde.

After a short discussion on particulars and ascertaining that the Bellapais villa had already been cleaned up for my occupancy, I rose and asked for the keys and directions to the villa.

"Oh, my son, Baris, will go up there with you to show the way," Layla said. And then she raised her voice toward the house, and her command for the appearance of her son produced a young man of nineteen or twenty years who was one of the most gorgeous youths I had ever seen. He was dark of complexion and had black, curly hair, but the eyes in his finely chiseled face were what caught and held my attention. They were sky blue. He was of medium height and had a lithe but sinewy build that would take longer than most Turkish men to turn to coarse thickness—or at least I hoped that would be the case, as he was a real heartbreaker.

He bore himself just as his mother did. I knew her to be Egyptian, of the stock that Durrell wrote of in his *Quartet*. And when I looked at her son again, I surmised that her genes must be prominent in him. Although he had the coloring of a Cypriot, indeed as Layla herself had, he didn't really seem to be one in origin with either the Greeks or the Turks who predominated on this island. I knew that there was a strong strain of the Italian here from the Venetian period, and even an older influence of the English from Richard the Lionhearted and the crusades. Perhaps some of these traits were fighting for recognition in this achingly handsome young man, I thought. Perhaps.

"I had planned to stay the weekend at the villa and not come back into Kyrenia, Ms. Ergun," I said to Layla. And I said it with much regret as I ached to be alone with his beautiful young man. "So, perhaps it would be best if you just gave me some directions to the villa, or your Baris will be trapped on the mountain without transport home."

"That is not a problem," Layla said. "He can come down with his cousins who live up there but who will be coming down here to work in the morning."

My small Mercedes convertible seemed claustrophobic as it chugged up the first incline above Kyrenia and toward Bellapais. I was sitting nearly hip-to-hip with a young man I already ached for, and the tenting of my trousers was probably signaling my interest. No, not probably. Obviously, considering what Baris said to me without the slightest embarrassment.

"My mother thinks you are much like that man, Taylor, who lived up at the villa a few years ago."

"Yes, that's what she said," I answered. "I have no idea why she said that."

"That Mr. Taylor let men make love to him," Baris said matter-of-factly. "It was well known throughout the area, and I'm told he was a handsome and generous man. The men flocked to him. I was just a boy when he left here, but even I heard of these things."

I drew in my breath and fought for control of the wheel, something I really needed to have on this narrow, upward-curved poor excuse for a road.

Baris continued as I felt the pressure of his thigh against mine. "I am no longer a boy, Mr. Henson. Are you like that man, Taylor, in that way? Do you let men make love to you?"

I was lost. "Yes," I said meekly, my voice pitched low enough that perhaps, just perhaps, he would not hear my response.

But Baris did hear my response, and by the time we entered the lower reaches of Bellapais, he had my fly open and his strong, calloused hand on my engorging cock. We shuffled directly to the terrace on the slope side of the villa when we reached the house, and Baris had me stripped and on my back on a lounger, my legs spread wide, his teeth worrying my nipples, and his manly piece driving home before I could catch my breath.

He was young and strong and virile and fucked me to completion repeatedly until dusk. I already was attracted to Mediterranean men, but this may have been the moment where Turkish men became a fetish for me. They made love with such a free exuberance, that I cried out in joy with each ejaculation.

When the cool wind began to flow more strongly and coldly up the mountain slope from the Mediterranean and across the stone terrace and I could see the first twinkly star appear in the clear sky, I nudged a peacefully snoring youth who had gone to sleep still buried deep inside me. I suggested that we find the bedroom, and he groggily came awake and said he'd give me a tour of the house and then he'd give me seven hard, thick inches again on a very strong double bed.

It was only then that I realized that his mother, Layla, had certainly known where her son would be spending the night.

After that, I withdrew to my Bellapais mountainside retreat whenever I could. And, with Baris smoothing the way, I enlarged my circle of men servicers until my days and nights in the Bellapais villa became a matter of hedonist habit. And Baris would play for us. He had a talent for picking out a tune on any stringed instrument and making it sing and making all who heard it drift off into sensuous dreaming.

Ahh, the days of drifting down to the Tree of Idleness in the square in the late afternoon and sitting ogling the local Turkish Cypriot men and letting them ogle me until I got that certain look from one I fancied. Then taking him up to my rented villa and letting him vigorously, joyously, and noisily fuck my brains out on a lounger under the sun on the terrace overlooking the Mediterranean.

As soon as that phrase had spun out from my thoughts, I knew that it was not my own thought but something I'd read somewhere. And then I remembered. I had started reading Mark Amalfi's book, *The Tree of Idleness*, as soon as I settled in the Durrell villa, and this and other phrases from that book had burned their images of compulsive "want" into my brain. I even knew how that phrase continued—and very soon after having read that in his book, I came to know the action itself. It had been as if the villa had whispered these words to me. And when I started going down to the Bellapais square to pick up a man for the night I was somehow sure I was following in Amalfi's footsteps—and possibly in the footsteps of other tenants of this villa. And maybe the villa itself had a hand in this obsession.

And then back down to the square in the twilight after dinner with those fairy lights in the olive trees around the fringe of the stone café terrace, and, in that soft light and twittering laughter of the Mediterranean men and wisps of strong Turkish tobacco drifting up, eyeing and being eyed until I got the certain look from one I fancied and took him back up to the villa and let him fuck me in long, slow, sweeping strokes on the terrace under the stars.

And maybe, if he was really, really beautiful and masterful, taking him back to my bed for a night of sleep broken by brief periods of wanton lust, waking to the feel of a hot poker at my hole and a wheedling whisper for permission at my ear and arching back to accept the homage of a throbbing need to be deep inside me. Breakfasting on the terrace by the small pool and then pulling him into the pool and wrapping my legs around his waist and letting the swirling water soften the rhythmic in and outing as I threw my head back and watched the morning Mediterranean light filter through the sighing branches of the olive trees and thought about my late afternoon visit to the Tree of Idleness café in the Bellapais square, already assessing which eyes I would respond to today.

Once I started reading Mark Amalfi's book, I returned to it again and again. I liked to read it sitting at the desk in the living room, as I had found a strange painting hanging over the desk that I always, somehow, linked to Amalfi's book. I suspected that it could be a Val Cramner. My cultural duties had included hosting several art exhibits over the years, and I had come to recognize the colors and brush strokes that marked a Cramner painting. They were becoming increasingly famous—and expensive—now. This was a strange example, though, if a true Cramner. It had been overpainted, part of it by a different, less talented painter, I was sure—and Cramner was famous for painting people.

This painting was of two empty café chairs on either side of a table, against a sun-drenched ochre-colored stone wall. I knew of the tragic story of Amalfi and Cramner, and as I sat at the desk and read Amalfi's words, my mind was drawn to the painting hanging above and I felt the sadness flowing off it. Often after I had read a bit, I found I wanted to write. But when I wrote, my pen wanted to write forbidden prose, words that I would not have wanted my name and position to be identified with, words that didn't press on me to be written anywhere else that I sat to compose other than this villa. And I found that to be sad as well.

Months went by, and my need for what Amalfi was writing about—and what my hand wanted to write about when I set pen to paper at the villa—had become an addiction. And sometimes I would need to bring more than one man back to the villa with me. Sometimes I had an itch that required more than one scratching. When I was resting before my trips down into the village square, I reread Durrell's *Alexandria Quartet* while stretched out in front of a fireplace on a loggia within view of the Mediterranean far below and slowly but surely became aware of the underlying sensuality of the work. And I wondered if I was seeing this because of my new insights into Durrell's masterwork or because of what the villa was coaxing me to see in it—as it may have enchanted Amalfi to see in it—or because of the constant stream of virile young men through my life.

It was in the fall of the year, still summer during the day in Cyprus, but softer and increasingly cooler in the evening. It was getting late on that particular evening, and none of the younger Turkish men seemed to be about in the coffee shop in the square. It already was past midnight, and I thought that I would be sleeping alone up in the rented villa this night. Only older, grizzly men were sitting around and drinking their Ouzo and smoking their pipes and Turkish cigarettes and giving me those leery looks.

They knew why I vacationed in Bellapais. They knew what went on at my rented villa up the winding cobble-stoned street from the square. They closed their eyes to it because I was Canadian and had money to give—and because it had gone on there before.

They also closed their eyes to it because this was tolerated—and almost expected—of Mediterranean men, going back to the ancient Greeks. Their history tolerated relations between men as well as—even alongside—relations of men and women. And as long as the man was the giver, the control, not the receptacle, nothing much was thought of it. Men had needs to be relieved; it didn't make them any less men to take another man in the local thinking—and certainly not a man who was not of their village.

When Baris was being particularly demonstrative toward me in public, I briefly feared that there would be trouble over this, that I might have stepped on some sort of taboo in taking up with one of their very young men, but, strangely enough, the men at the Tree of Idleness treated Baris almost as a foreigner as well. I wondered if this was because his mother wasn't Cypriot. But she had been here almost forever, I would have thought—

and the owner of the Tree of Idleness himself was her brother-in-law. But then I supposed this was just the way of insular Mediterranean island environments like this one. Maybe Baris would never be accepted as well—although those lounging in the café in the late evenings certainly seemed to appreciate his expert playing of their native stringed instruments.

As I pondered this one evening when the café seemed incongruously almost deserted of young men—Baris not even being there—I grew tired of waiting for the hunt to begin and spun some coins out on the table. As I rose, Sami, the shop owner, drifted by me and warned me in whispered tones that the younger men had just returned from a football game, where the local Kyrenia team had lost to the arch rival Salamis team. He whispered in hurried, clipped words that they were in the inner courtyard of the café now, ordering brandy to top the wine they doused themselves with at the game.

There were six of them, he said, and all but two of those he named I had enjoyed in my villa courtyard during this three-day weekend visit. He said they were in a mean frame of mind and that one had mentioned to the others that I was at the café, and he had made certain "suggestions." Sami thought that I should leave by the north exit and double around to my street leading up the mountain at the west exit. I thought of the six men. I had enjoyed the four who have fucked me already, and I ached for the other two, who were the biggest and most handsome and macho of the lot. And I had had a fair amount of wine.

To the surprise of Sami, I rose and walked straight toward the west exit, the path going past the entrance into the inner courtyard. I did not make it past the entrance. In my passing, strong hands came out of the darkness and pulled me into the inner courtyard. My clothes were ripped from my body. I put up a half-hearted defense and was slapped hard across my face for the effort and slammed down on my back on a wooden café table.

I tried to rise, but I was backhanded again and fell back on the tabletop. Hands were handling me everywhere. Insistent, frenzied hands. There was drunken laughter and sneered talk in slurred Turkish mixed with a bit of English. I clearly heard the words "fuck" and "sweet hole" come up again and again, always meeting with raucous laughter and menacing tones of hurried, furtive whisperings. I could tell from the jabberings that they were arguing among themselves but that the two bigger men, the ones who had not tasted me yet, took ascendance. The four others stationed themselves at my limbs, holding me down and stretching me out in a sacrificial X. Brandy was being poured over my body and the biggest of the Turks took a mouthful from the bottle, gave me a possessive leer, and dipped his head below my belly, between my legs, and I felt the stinging wetness of the alcohol being spit into my canal, stopped from escaping there from by clamping lips and searching tongue. I had men's lips and teeth all over my body then, tonguing and nipping the film of brandy, flesh, and my nipples and mouth.

My arousal was reaching new heights; the very uncertainty and threat of the situation was exhilarating to me. I was trembling with anticipation.

The other bruiser who had not yet known me was above my head, which now dropped over the end of the table, well in position for him to saddle up to me and push a bigger dick than the four who had already fucked me past my lips. He filled me and started to pump me there just as the largest cock of all thrust into my canal and took my mind off all other points of assault with its fury and filling.

I spit out the second one's cock just long enough to make a plea, borne not from my fear and noncompliance but from my desire to keep my assaulters' alcohol-drenched sense of completely taking keenly edged.

"Help, help! He is forcing me. Oh, he is soooo big. No, no, Arghhhh. Please, give me time. Please release me. No, no, you're splitttting me! Ahhhhhhhhh. Ohhhhhh. Help! Help me." Other fat fingers joined the huge tool working inside me.

"Oh god, not those too. No, no, not that. Ohhhhhhh. Moannnnnn. Help! Help me. Whimmmperr." I was crying for help, pushing my assailants to a frenzy, and I'm sure we could be heard by the other men in the outer courtyard. But the only response was that someone turned up the radio on which a woman was wailing some Turkish song of being done wrong by her man that fed her determination to return to him.

I lifted my head as the bruiser who had been face fucking me stopped at a signal to take his turn inside my canal, and I saw Sami, the café owner standing in the shadows of the entrance of the inner court. I cried out to him for help, maintaining my role in this taking, knowing that he was beyond intervening, but he remained standing there. As the biggest dick pulled out of me and I had two or more fingers digging inside me, I was able to focus on Sami, who had his cock out of his trousers and was pulling on it as he watched me being taken by the drunken, keyed-up, disappointed fans of the losing football game.

I cried out as the second cock was thrust inside me, pumping rapidly in the lubricant of the cum left by the first one. There must have been fears that my cries would go beyond the courtyard even over the wailing of the Turkish songstress on the radio, because I was roughly backhanded across the face again, and before I could regain my breath, a small flag of the losing team was stuffed in my mouth to gag me.

After the second of the assaulters had quickly unloaded inside me, I was roughly turned on my belly, and I serviced the four remaining drunken Turks, two of them together in a fucking that turned me woozy. As I was slowly blacking out, the one who took me first started his second fucking. He had his fist buried in my hair, pulling my head back toward him, with my back arched in full extension and my arms still being held out from my body by two of the others. He was muttering phrases, and kept repeating "fuck Salamis" over and over again.

It was light when I awakened. The room was strange to me, but through the French doors, I could see what must be the inner courtyard of the café. Sami was sitting beside me on the single, rough wood bed with thin down-filled mattress I was resting on. My muscles felt like I have run a marathon and my head was throbbing, but I otherwise felt at peace and satiated. Sami was apologizing to me in low whispers as he stroked my forehead with a cloth. I still was naked, and I was sure the clothes I wore to the café were rags now.

I asked for water, and it was only then, as I tried to reach for it, that I found both of my wrists are loosely tied by leather straps to the bedposts. Sami lifted my head to the water cup, and

I sputtered as I drank it. As soon as I stopped gagging from the water, I started asking why I was bound.

But Sami just continued to look stricken and whispering apologies. He then stood, and stripped down his trousers, and I saw that he was hard as a rock and of prodigious proportions.

He walked around to the bottom of the bed and pulled my butt down to the edge, which stretched my bound arms out above my head. He had his bulbous mushroom cap resting at my entrance when he made his only half-angry flare of a statement. It was in broken Turkish and English, but I got the gist of it. He said something about his village and foreign whores and of my walking by the entrance of the inner courtyard despite his warning and wanting what I was getting. And then he thrust inside me and fucked me in long slidings that went on for some time before he was finished.

Spent, Sami pulled out of me, wiped himself off with a handkerchief. He then walked over to the open French doors and muttered something to someone outside.

For the next hour, a succession of the older men who had been in the café's outer courtyard the night before filed in, singly, all without trousers, and fucked me to their completions. I think there were five in all. I would not have made a fuss when they were done with me even if I had wanted to—the last one who assaulted me was the village police chief.

They simply let me go then. Still incongruously apologizing, Sami supplied me with a cotton shirt and trousers that fit reasonably well, and I gingerly hobbled my way up the winding cobble-stoned street to my rented villa in a bowlegged gait.

That night, a victim of my urges, I walked back down to the square in the twilight after dinner with those fairy lights in the olive trees around the fringe of the stone café terrace. And, I sat at a table in the shadows, just beyond that soft light and twittering laughter of the Mediterranean men and wisps of strong Turkish tobacco drifting up, eyeing and being eyed until the biggest young man of the previous evening came to the café. Not fully drunk tonight. Supremely surprised at seeing me there. Perhaps a little sheepish about the drunken gangbang after the previous day's disappointment at the football stadium. But I had

55

hoped he would be here tonight. I gave him the certain look until I got the certain look back, and then I took him back up to the villa and let him fuck me in long, slow, sweeping strokes on the terrace under the stars, followed by a night-long test of his virility in my bed—a test he passed with flying colors and ever-hard, thick, and long dick.

It took me several months to come to grips with my addiction. I begged to be sent away from this paradise of an island. When my transfer came to Indonesia, I was almost too far gone to pull away from the clutches the Bellapais villa had on me. But I will never say I regretted the experience or that I will never return.

Chapter 5: Munro Possession

by Sabb

In 1968 a friend in England had suggested I rent Lawrence Durrell's villa in Bellapais, Turkish Cyprus. It had been three years since the troubles between the Greeks and the Turks on the island had developed into a low-level insurgency, but thus far the largely expatriate artist's community in the mountainside village of Bellapais had been spared of any sense of personal danger.

My friend was a writer, and he had said, "There are places that can inspire a man, and having read Lawrence Durrell's, *Bitter Lemons* and *The Alexandria Quartet*, I am sure that his villa on Cyprus will be full of inspiration. And I have heard it's available to rent. Go there, Simon. For me."

I could hardly refuse him, as I knew he himself was longing to take Durrell's villa. But he was tied to cold damp London by a sick wife, three small children, and a demanding job with *The Times Literary Supplement*.

I had followed through on the villa, mainly because I had always had a soft spot for my literary friend. And I'd had the villa for only a month when I wrote to him, saying that, yes, it was full of inspiration, though perhaps not the inspiration he imagined. There was no literary inspiration there for me, but there was an immense amount of sexual discovery. And I said sincerely that I wished he were there to share it with me. And for six months I was ecstatically inspired by it until I was suddenly forced to leave. And my time in Turkey was also up soon after and I returned to England.

Then, last year I had finally come back to Turkish Cyprus. I was semiretired, and was now idling my days away in my apartment in the old part of Kyrenia, when I wasn't working hard, lecturing on the Middle East at Oxford. I had always longed to return to Durrell's villa, but it had never been vacant when I enquired, until recently, when I had seen Layla Ergun, Lawrence's old friend and Bellapais villa landlady, on the other side of the square and crossed over and asked her about it on a whim.

Now I was returning from England for the winter, and with his sick wife long gone, and his children at university, my literary friend would shortly be coming to visit for a fortnight with his lover, and the villa would be my gift to them.

The plane had got me to the Ercan airport on time and I collected my car and drove straight to Kyrenia, glad that I was home and immediately I took the old familiar walk along the jetty wall, around the harbor side and nearly to the walls of Kyrenia castle, a peculiar harbor defense castle of a hulking Lusignan fortress that was constructed around an existing Byzantine castle of Richard the Lionhearted vintage. The cafés across the road were already starting to fill up as I wandered lazily by, savoring my return, and occasionally I saw a familiar face among the patrons and nodded slightly to them.

The old town was the same, but slightly different, because even in the three months I had been away, it had subtly changed. It lay nestled by the harbor as it had for centuries, but it now sat against a constantly expanding backdrop of modern holiday flats and villas climbing the sharp-peaked Kyrenia-range mountainside behind. And each time I returned there were more pale-skinned European faces in the crowd.

From the balcony of the British Club café, a familiar, rich baritone voice called out to me, and I crossed the cobble-stoned road and climbed the stairs to join Mustafa, the nephew of my landlady, Layla, and be embraced by him. He had aged into a solid bull of a man, all heavy shoulders and thick neck and belly, the beautiful solid man of twenty-two, the renowned Turkish folk song singer and baglama player I had once known, lost beneath the intervening years of contentment and good living. But as the body had grown, so had the humor and friendship, and we embraced with affection.

And as we embraced, I smelt the familiar warm scent of him and closed my eyes and was taken back to when we had first known each other in that fateful year of 1968, twenty years before. When I had come to the island and the villa alone, escaping from the crowded city whenever I could. But not spending my time there alone.

Ahh, the days of drifting down to the Tree of Idleness in the square in the late afternoon and sitting ogling the local Turkish Cypriot men and letting them ogle me until I got that certain look from one I fancied. Then taking him up to my rented villa and letting him vigorously, joyously, and noisily fuck my brains out on a lounger under the sun on the terrace overlooking the Mediterranean.

And then back down to the square in the twilight after dinner with those fairy lights in the olive trees around the fringe of the stone café terrace, and, in that soft light and twittering laughter of the Mediterranean men and wisps of strong Turkish tobacco drifting up, eyeing and being eyed until I got the certain look from one I fancied and took him back up to the villa and let him fuck me in long, slow, sweeping strokes on the terrace under the stars.

And maybe, if he was really, really beautiful and masterful, taking him back to my bed for a night of sleep broken by brief periods of wanton lust, waking to the feel of a hot poker at my hole and a wheedling whisper for permission at my ear and arching back to accept the homage of a throbbing need to be deep inside me. Breakfasting on the terrace by the small pool and then pulling him into the pool and wrapping my legs around his waist and letting the swirling water soften the rhythmic in and outing as I threw my head back and watched the morning Mediterranean light filter through the sighing branches of the olive trees and thought about my late afternoon visit to the Tree of Idleness café in the Bellapais square, already assessing which eyes I would respond to today.

Ahhh, idyllic days. Days of youth. No, even then, in the beginning, I hadn't been that young. I had been a thirty-five-year-old man working in Turkey and needing to escape.

"You look good," Mustafa said, holding me at arm's length, smiling and nodding. "And the villa. It is yours for two weeks?" he asked.

"Yes. But not for me, I'm renting it for my friends," I replied, smiling foolishly.

"Ahh. I don't understand why you want to rent that old place, when you could have had a big new flat, or a house like mine. My brother has built many good villas; he has many for sale," he added enthusiastically.

"All you think of is new," I replied sharply, wishing that more of the old island remained, the ancient ochre-colored stone walls, the old houses with their heavy wooden doors, hidden lush courtyard gardens, and cool dim whitewashed interiors, the inconvenient but shaded winding lanes.

"OK. OK. You foreigners," he said with a smile, not understanding what outsiders might see in his island's past, "I'll see you later. Tomorrow," he added, leaving me.

But then he turned back and his face was sad. "You probably don't even remember him now. Kemal. Do you remember Kemal? The musician? He played in the cafés with Layla's son Baris; he's the one who discovered and encouraged Baris's talent with the instruments. Well, Kemal died in a car accident last week," Mustafa said and shook his head slowly "So much trouble for you both. So long ago," he added sadly, before moving off to answer a call from an English customer inside.

They were everywhere now the English retirees, and standing where he had left me, I watched him hurry back into the dull cool interior of the old-style café. For a few moments I had no idea who he was talking about, who Kemal was. But my mind spun through memories and suddenly the name Kemal clicked into place, and I stood, stunned, as the past washed over me.

Oh God. Kemal, how could I have forgotten him. I felt ill as the memories of those months twenty years before overwhelmed me.

I would go down to the square in Bellapais after lunch, or in the evenings, and wander into the familiar old-fashioned street café operated by Sami and named after the tree that shaded its open-air tables. The Tree of Idleness—some sort of banyan-type local tree with wide-spreading branches, and beneath it there are always a variety of Turkish Cypriot men drinking coffee in small cups and Efes beer in brown bottles and idling their time away. And I would sit up on one of the stools by the counter, waiting to be ogled, to be eyed off, and then later to be possessed by the man of my choosing.

I had seen it as no more than part of escaping from my demanding work and obligations in the city, an escape into an indulgent place of timeless pleasure. But then one day I had been possessed in a way I had never imagined.

Yes. One day I had walked down the winding cobbled lane to the square without realizing that I was taking the walk that marked the end of my island days as clearly as anything ever could. The café was busy on that day, and Sami's son, Mustafa, the handsome, smiling twenty-two-year-old honey skinned, godlike youth, who had eyed me off himself more than once, had to clear someone from a stool so I had somewhere to sit. And I looked about in mild surprise at the crowd, but with no real curiosity. There were even more good-looking young men there that day than usual, and it was that I had come there for. I had felt the heat in me rise and I'd been happy.

At first I hardly even noticed that quite a few of the younger men were clustered in a laughing, murmuring group to one side, arms linked about each others' shoulders and their bodies moving with the talk.

But then several turned to look at me and I smiled back, realizing I must have become the topic of conversation. Then most in the group were turning to look at me with looks of lust, curiosity, a few even of dislike, before the bodies moved aside so that those sitting at the table in the shadows behind them could see me too. There was much quiet laughter and whispering, and I felt the thrill of knowing that they were admiring me, and sure that two of them, who I remembered taking home at different times, were showing by their smiling looks and whispers how good it had been.

A couple gave me that certain look and I returned it, but there was some more talk, and one of the men seated at the table in the shadows stood up, and the group was making a humming noise and the looks had turned to different ones. Not unpleasant, not lustful, different. They were the looks of men on the eve of the big game who know their football team is certain to win.

The man at the table stepped through them, and I saw him clearly for the first time. He was giving me a look, but it was not the usual one. He was young and slim and proud, but his look was almost a shy one, his huge dark eyes giving an impression of something serious yet timeless. At odds with the murmurings of the group around him and with his own posture.

I heard someone suck in a breath behind me, and knew it was Mustafa. I had no idea who the young man coming toward me was, but he obviously mattered in the village, so I made an effort to look friendly and harmless.

He stepped up to me and said, "We go," his huge dark eyes holding mine briefly, and the look was one of me being politely ordered, and I sensed I had no choice whatever I wanted.

Fortunately, he was good looking in his own brooding way, and I mentally shrugged and stood up and smiled to his friends as I left the café, with my companion leading the way. I heard laughter and shouts behind us; very different to the normal casual way I left.

He knew my villa in the upper reaches of Bellapais and led us there along the lane and at the heavy door into the courtyard, just walked in, knowing it wouldn't be locked. Inside, he looked around briefly before he continued into the house, glancing into the central living room and stopping at the door of the bedroom to the side of the entrance, turning to me suddenly.

"You are English?" he asked in a deep, honey smooth, almost accentless voice.

He was no ordinary island youth, speaking English poorly. Cyprus having long been a British colony, those native to the island often spoke English, but not always well. But this youth obviously had originated elsewhere.

In the shadow inside the villa, his eyes were gleaming, and all I could think was what big dark bedroom eyes he had and what beautiful long lashes. The sort of young man I might choose to fuck myself the odd time I wanted that. When I needed to be the possessor. To own beauty and youth.

"Yes," I replied.

"And your name," he asked, his eyes not leaving my face.

"Simon. Simon Munro."

"Kemal," he said, a small smile passing over his mouth as he reached out a hand and shook mine. "How do you do?"

"Very well," I said smiling back, the tension suddenly gone.

We were standing in the doorway into the bedroom, with its French windows opening on to the terrace overlooking the sea, and he walked calmly past me and toward the bed that I had made up with fresh sheets that morning. And it flitted through my mind that if we were going to have each other, I wanted it to be like that, on fresh linen, in the shady room, on a perfect day, overlooking the Mediterranean.

"So I fuck you now," he said, which almost made me laugh, as he didn't look as if he was particularly interested in doing it.

But then I realized why he was there. He was required to do this because of who he was, whether he particularly wanted to or not. And I suddenly resented it that he wasn't particularly interested, when I could have been looking at another man who was.

"Can I get you a drink?" I asked, thinking we could just fill some time and he could return to the café and give his opinion of "the Englishman, the foreigner," without us actually having to do anything.

I was no good when sex was a chore. I saw myself getting naked and lying on the bed with my legs wide waiting for him to fuck me like some bored whore, and smiled to myself as I vaguely wondered if I should "think of England" like some Victorian virgin, as he plowed me.

"No," he replied, pulling his shirt free of his pants and starting to unbutton it.

He was not beautiful in the usual Turkish Cypriot way; there was something much too lean and elegant about him. But the body he revealed as he undid his shirt was unexpectedly muscular, full of flowing lean shape and hardness and strength. One I could definitely work up some interest in, I thought, as I also began to strip off, not sure how to go with him and just following his lead.

We were both quickly naked and he had given me his second big surprise. His cock was already half hard and was obviously going to get to a good size. The head was big and flared, and the shaft was already long and bulgingly full. His balls were high and almost small.

I sat on the bed while he stood there stroking himself, getting harder and larger as I moved into the middle and lay back. He made no move to come to me. Just stood there playing with himself and watching me intently. I looked back at him as I stroked myself and lifted my legs and fingered some lube into my own hole. But, however odd the situation was, he was turning me on in some strange way. There was nothing soft then about those big dark eyes of his in spite of his odd shyness. They were more like the eyes of a huge cat fixed on its prey, in total control. And that look was turning me on hugely.

"You are ready now," he observed quietly, smiling in a satisfied way, seeing my eyes move down and fix on his now fully engorged, long, thick tool.

I nodded, and I truly *was* ready.

He moved onto the bed and between my thighs, and I wanted to scream for him to fuck me—for the slow quiet control he held me in to break into the instinctive, wild thrusting of fucking and coming. I wanted to be released from his control, even if only to fist myself to ejaculation.

But instead, he stayed calm and unhurried, his eyes fixing me and freezing me still, as he guided the big flared head of his cock to my hole and pushed. It was painful immediately, I wasn't as ready as I needed to be to take him easily, and I grunted as he entered me, feeling like an observer until he pushed in deeper. He was splitting me, but I felt unable to do any more than look into his big eyes and accept him into me, grunting and whimpering quietly as he opened me. Until his flared head rubbed across my prostrate, when I suddenly felt freed and arched back and wrapped my legs about his hips and yelled, "Fuck me, fuck me," knowing that as completely unexpected as it was, he was going to give me exactly what I wanted—an overpowering ride that filled me completely.

My cry was the signal he needed, and he bottomed inside me forcefully, a burst of pain shooting through me making me scream again, "No, no," and leaving me whimpering and crying out as he began to plow me with huge deep strokes that had me writhing and telling him to stop, that he was hurting me so.

But he didn't stop. And I didn't really want him to.

He kept on and on. Slow and fast, slow and shallow. Several times I looked into his face and his eyes were still those of some great cat with its prey being batted playfully between its paws, and I moaned as the pain turned to pleasure, and I was gripping the bed head and bucking my hips to match his thrusting and pulling him in deeper.

I came early on, cream streaking up my belly to my chest and staying there to dry as he continued to plow me, my legs pulling him in as I moaned for more of what he was doing to me. When he finally came, it was deep inside me, and my thighs held him tight as I felt the heat of him flooding me.

I came again, then slowly released my legs from about his hips and lay there looking up at him, completely possessed by him and expecting him to pull out, calmly dress, and leave. But he didn't, not at first, he stayed there buried inside me, and I looked up at him and locked eyes with him, pleased that his big dark eyes were telling me he was satisfied. He stayed buried until his soft cock slipped out and I felt his cream dribble out behind it and run down my crack.

He pushed my right thigh back to my side and, with a finger of his right hand, rubbed the leaking cum around my asshole, making me moan. Then he wiped the cream over my nipples, the first time he had touched me there. Then he pressed the finger between my lips and I sucked off the taste of him. I shivered, realizing that he had symbolically taken total possession of me. And I lay there still, watching him as he got off the bed and calmly dressed, but when he was done, he threw me my clothes and I dressed for him as he watched. I felt like a visitor in his house the way he looked at me.

But it was erotic too, and I wanted it. The way he looked at me.

Then he was gone. Thinking about him afterwards, I thought he must be in his early twenties. The lean body and big eyes had made me think he was younger, but he had acted far older, yet I was sure he was aged far younger than the assurance he seemed born with had implied. I took a glass of wine out on to the veranda and found I was shaking as I settled down to drink it.

In the evening I went down to the café eagerly, feeling myself trembling and my cock filling as I entered the square and then made my way through the tables to the bar, feeling the men's eyes on me and hearing the mutterings and laughter in the clear warm night.

I took my seat on a stool, and Mustafa brought me a beer. Icy and refreshing. I had drunk half of it, when a beautiful man gave me that look, and I wanted to run up to the villa immediately with him. Or better, do it right there in front of the other customers. Then someone sat next to him and they were both eyeing me. Then they turned away. And I was abandoned for the night. Finally, I walked home alone and rationalized that I was leaving the next morning, to return to Istanbul and my research, and had a lot of work to do when I got back.

But that night I dreamed, and the dream was of Kemal and in the dream I ached for him and he appeared and roughly pushed me into positions in which I could watch him taking me vigorously, and I was begging him to take me and woke with my cream on the sheets.

The next weekend I was increasingly jittery and dry mouthed as the ferry approached the island. I disembarked in a rush and drove up to the villa to drop my bag before heading to the square and the Tree of Idleness café. And it was too early when I rushed in. There was hardly anyone there, and Mustafa was still slowly opening up. And I wanted to know, but couldn't ask directly.

I talked small talk, then said casually "Those young men who were here the other afternoon. Do they come here often?" Mustafa shrugged and moved away, ignoring me.

I wandered around the main part of the old village. Even then it was growing, stretched for quite a distance up a shallow valley between the hills not far from the busy town of Kyrenia, but there were only a couple of small blocks of new apartments on the hill directly behind the square. The rest was straggly goat pasture, a few small sheds and a lot of rocks. I had never seen Kemal before the previous Saturday, and I didn't see him anywhere that day either. I finally gave up looking for him and made my way back up to my villa in the dusk to get ready to go to the café for the evening.

When I arrived at the villa and entered the courtyard, I saw I had left a light on inside and the sound of a guitar being played floated out on the night air, but I was sure I hadn't left the radio on.

I wandered cautiously into the entry and stepped nervously up to my bedroom door, wary of what I might find there, and looked in. But it was him, Kemal, sitting naked on my bed, gazing at me broodingly as his fingers worked the strings of the guitar resting across his thighs. Then his eyes dropped to the instrument and his fingers moved over the strings as he continued to play. I soon realized that he played well. And as he finished one tune and started another, I knew he played much more than well.

He had me riveted, and his playing became more and more sensual and complex, his hands, with their long beautiful fingers, seeming to be part of the guitar. He looked up at me again. "Undress," he whispered. And as I undressed he watched me with his brooding look of concentration as he played and I removed my clothes to the music.

As I undressed, I moved to his music, touching myself in response to it, running my hands over my skin. Pinching my nipples and stroking my manhood as I removed my clothes and lay them neatly aside, wanting him to see me and want me. The house was right for that; the room was right, the light was right, I was a creature of lust, displaying myself for my audience. Showing my heat.

All I wanted was those long supple fingers exploring me and playing a tune on me. My body was shivering and my cock standing ready as I finished my display and stood there naked, his big dark eyes and his music caressing me better than my hands could. I wanted him to take me roughly, violently, and I moved closer, stroking myself, seeing his eyes move to my tool and rest there as he played more slowly and sensually, and I stroked myself. I wanted him to fuck me while he played and couldn't understand it was impossible.

I came with a huge shudder, cum riding up my belly and chest in bursts and he stopped playing suddenly and set the guitar aside. I fell to my knees between his spread thighs. He was already hard and dripping precum as I took his cock up and fed it to my lips. If I hadn't already come I would have then, just from discovering that he had been hard and dripping behind his guitar, as I had stroked myself off to his eyes and music.

I had barely got the taste of him and cupped and weighed his balls in my hand before he was lifting me and pushing me onto the bed on my knees and I knelt and widened my thighs for him dropping my head to the pillow.

"Fuck me," I begged him, reaching back to spread lube around my hole, his fingers taking over and working it inside me.

I was still young and was hard again as I moaned and moved my hips to fuck myself on his fingers, my free hand stroking my own cock as he was palming my belly, holding me steady, ready for him.

He entered me more easily this time, and I was moving with him and moaning from the beginning, not controlled by his eyes, and the look in them, as I had been on the first night. But he came quickly and I needed more of him. I rolled over and knelt before him and began to lick at his body, but he pulled back frowning.

I looked up at him, at his serious look, "Don't think so much," I said.

He looked back at me uncertainly, and I realized that in what we were doing, he was incredibly naïve. That I was the first man he had fucked. Stupidly, I thought how could I not have known that immediately. Because, the first time he had controlled me so easily and I had not been thinking of anything.

I leant in again more gently and played each of his erect nipples with my lips, then moved my mouth up and to his neck, his ears, his lips, wanting to hear him moan. He was reluctant to kiss, but I teased his mouth and finally he relaxed, and I darted my tongue in between the pink fleshy pads of his lips. But just enough to run along them before I moved my head down again and ran my lips over his chest, and down, playing at his belly, nuzzling his pubes and his treasure chest, nuzzling his half hard cock into my mouth. His hands gripped my head, as I knelt bent over before him, and I heard a faint noise escape him. I released his cock and took his balls into my mouth, sucking on them one at a time, and he definitely moaned.

When he was long and hard again, he pushed me back and I rested my feet on his shoulders, opening myself up for him. This time it was him who lubed up my hole, though it barely needed it, still being open and slick with his cum from earlier.

His long flexible fingers exploring inside me hit the right spot. "There, yes," I gasped, wanting him to know he had rubbed over something I wanted rubbed over. "Again."

He was a fast learner, and I saw a small smile cross his face as he fingered my ass and my cock hardened and dribbled for him as I moaned encouragement.

Then I was looking down and watching him feed his manhood slowly into me, knowing I could never get enough of it.

Kemal gripped my thighs as he plowed me, and I ran my hands over his belly and chest. We came together, him pulling out this time and his cock jerking and spouting cream over my belly and chest as mine did. He locked his eyes on mine as we both recovered, my feet still on his shoulders. Then he lent in and kissed me briefly.

"I will be back tomorrow," he said, kissing me when he left.

But I didn't see him again that weekend. I waited, and on Monday morning I took the last ferry I could back to the city of Mersin on the Turkish mainland.

When I went to buy a ticket on the Island ferry the next Friday afternoon, I was told it was full. I argued, and eventually the manager made them sell me a ticket, but I knew something was up.

When I arrived at the island, I was sworn at and my car spat on by the deckhand as I drove off the ferry, and I hurried up to my villa, worried about what may have happened. When I got there, I was relieved to find that things seemed normal, and I unlocked the doors and hurried through the courtyard and into the house to find that it was just as I had left it.

But I had barely finished inspecting the villa when I heard a car pull up outside and the sound of footsteps.

I walked back out to the courtyard and saw three men coming toward me. One was English, the other two Turkish, all big solid men, two older and a younger taller leaner one, and the youngest one was holding an Uzi slanted across his body. They stopped, and the Englishman stepped forward.

"You will be on the next ferry," he said, "And you will not be back. Ever."

"What's happened?" I asked.

But they just stared at me venomously, and the Uzi was lifted. I would have run if I'd had anywhere to run to, but the only way out of the villa was through the courtyard door they were blocking. Meanwhile, another car had pulled up outside, and there were fast hurried footsteps, and Layla Ergun, my landlady, was suddenly framed in the entrance from the lane.

"He is leaving, Mr. Winfield," she said loudly. "I will help him get his bags. Please wait outside."

Layla was far from her usual calm self. "Wait outside, please," she repeated loudly.

"I blame you for this Layla," the Englishman said, " you encourage these men to come here, and now it's Kemal who is being led astray."

"Things will be all right. He will settle down."

"Sooner, if this one is gone," the young Turk with the Uzi said.

"It will pass," Layla replied pleadingly, "It will pass. Please wait outside."

The men went grudgingly out to stand in the lane just beyond the doorway.

"You must go," Layla said, running into the house and pulling my bags out of the cupboards. "I am sorry. Kemal. . . ah, his grandfather is . . . is high up in Turkey, and he is the only grandson. And the Mr. Winfield, the so proper angry Englishman, is his uncle here for the engagement that Kemal called off last week, saying he did not want to be with a woman. And they blame you."

I threw what I could into the bags I had there, and we carried them out to my car and put them in the boot, under the malevolent gaze of the three strangers.

I knew enough about the way the island really worked to be afraid, and I left what didn't fit into my bags and let myself be helped to leave.

When I tried to ask Layla what had happened to Kemal, she only said "Not now, not now. There is nothing I can do. Foreigners. All foreigners."

I drove myself to the ferry, only stopping in Bellapais to slip into Sami's café in the square below the villa and grab Mustafa frantically by the arm.

"What has happened to Kemal?" I asked him, fearfully. "Is Kemal all right?"

Mustafa looked at me, half sorry and half frightened. "Let go," he said angrily, shaking my hand off his arm. "You took the wrong one home. These English and the old-fashioned Turks . . . ," he said. "You have caused big trouble for him, and for you."

"Who is Kemal?" I asked .

"Go. Go," was all he said, pushing me roughly out onto the street.

I came back from my memories, staring blankly into the gloom of Mustafa's current British Club café near Kyrenia harbor, remembering how I had caught the next ferry back to Mersin, shattered that I might never see the villa, or the island again. Or Kemal. And not only might I never see them again, I had felt I was cut off forever from any escape from the impersonal bustle of the Turkish mainland. I had lost my private paradise, as well as the dominating lover who played so passionately on the guitar.

After years of thinking about, and pining for the carefree Turkish Cypriot way of life I had discovered in Lawrence Durrell's villa, I had finally returned to Northern Cyprus twenty years later and renewed that love affair.

But I had never seen Kemal again or thought of him till now.

Chapter 6: Taylor Possession

by Shabbu

When I was young, I had a different attitude. I wanted it all, and I had it all, but it was like a right then, a god-given right, and I found it easily. I never quite lost it, and now I have it all again, but no, not like I did back then.

Not like the days when I was young and I first found my escape on the island, in the Bellapais villa. A young man's pleasure and strength between the thighs of the lovely Layla, who watched over the villa I was renting and who did so, in those sweet mid '60s years in the isolated artists' village paradise of Bellapais, between my sheets.

And, randy young soul that I then was, also the men. The melting Turkish men. Ahh, the days of drifting down to the Tree of Idleness in the square in the late afternoon and sitting ogling the local Turkish Cypriot men and letting them ogle me until I got that certain look from one I fancied. Then taking him up to my rented villa and letting him vigorously, joyously, and noisily fuck my brains out on a lounger under the sun on the terrace overlooking the Mediterranean.

Or down to the square in the twilight after dinner, with those fairy lights in the olive trees around the fringe of the café's stone terrace. And, in that soft light, hearing the twittering laughter of the Mediterranean men and watching the wisps of strong Turkish tobacco smoke drifting up, as I was eyeing and being eyed. Until I got that certain look from someone I fancied and took him back up to the villa and let him fuck me in long, slow, sweeping strokes as I lay back on my lounger on the terrace under the stars.

And maybe, if he was really, really beautiful and masterful, taking him back to my bed for a night of sleep broken by brief periods of wanton lust, waking to the feel of a hot poker at my hole and a wheedling whisper for permission at my ear. Me sighing "Yes" and arching back to accept the homage of his throbbing need to be deep inside me.

Breakfasting on the terrace by the small pool. Then pulling him into the pool and wrapping my legs around his waist and letting the swirling water soften the rhythmic in and outing as I threw my head back and watched the morning Mediterranean light filter through the sighing branches of the olive trees. Thinking then about my late afternoon visit to the Tree of Idleness café in the Bellapais square, already assessing which eyes I would respond to that day.

Then that had ended, unexpectedly, as those seemingly endless days of youthful perfect pleasure do. Unfortunately, they decided to have a civil war on Cyprus and carve it up when the mainland Turkish troops invaded and the Greek mainland troops failed to respond. Abandoning my villa with nothing but the clothes on my back, I scrambled up and over the Kyrenia range ridgeline, as Turkish paratroopers glided down into the meadow below the cliffside abbey walls. And I stumbled into the temporary safety of Nicosia along with streams of sobbing Greeks, being displaced for decades from their ancestral homes.

For a long time I couldn't get back to that part of the island either, even though my foreign status enabled me to enter there through Turkey. I tried briefly living in the Greek sector, teaching composition at the English School. But even this, a job I had been lucky to acquire, only made me ache for my favorite part of the island—my rented villa perched above the Bellapais abbey. Every day I faced a composition class, I recalled the author who had preceded me in the villa, Lawrence Durrell, and I ached for the ecstasy I had found there. The fulfillment that Durrell had enjoyed there at the tip of his pen was a fulfillment that I also had enjoyed, as nowhere else, in the arms of the

Egyptian temptress, Layla, and at the tip of an endless succession of Turkish Cypriot cocks.

I returned to Sydney, where the island became a memory, and I collected Mediterranean and Turkish lovers in Australia instead. And I found many of the same attitudes to sex that I had found on that small island still hung about the men I took home and enjoyed being fucked by, there on that much bigger island continent lost in Asia. But I was never to attain the sexual fulfillment and satisfaction that I had found in my Bellapais villa. And my life was spoiled; Australia could no longer satisfy my wants and needs.

Then I had the opportunity to return to northern Cyprus, and I was in two minds about it. Torn by knowing that returning to the paradise of our past is so often a mistake, and that instead of regaining paradise, we lose the perfect memory of it.

So I hesitated. But the pull was strong, and in the end, I said, "For six months." Six months to see if I could recover that timeless sense of pleasure.

I returned, twenty-five years after I had left, via Istanbul, to an airport I would never have recognized and drove a hire car along roads that hadn't been there when I left. But when I arrived in Kyrenia, the town I had known, it was to find it recognizable, the old part hardly changed at all. And when I drove nervously out to the village where I had spent my weekends, I found it familiar enough to make my heart race and my cock stiffen in anticipation. Then I drove cautiously up the familiar, narrow, steep, stone-bedded road to where I had rented the small villa I had spent my weekends and free time at. And it was there still too. I stopped the car and sat there looking at it, wondering. Remembering.

It had been added to, a large pergola and a second story over half of the central section. But they hadn't spoiled the setting or the view. When I looked down from where I was on the mountainside, I saw the changes more clearly. Units in small complexes scattered up the side of the hill behind the village in search of the sea views and a cool breeze. But my old Bellapais villa remained apart, near the summit of its spiky mountaintop overlooking the Mediterranean.

"It's a mistake to try to relive the past," I muttered to myself. Still, the villa drew me to it. If I told anyone among the English-speaking hangers on in Cyprus of this attraction, they would have told me that this was because this was the villa where the British novelist Lawrence Durrell had penned his *Alexandria Quartet*. But that held no attraction in and of itself to me. The pull of the villa for me was totally sexual. I had never felt more sexually alive than I had felt while living there. Whenever I had brought Layla or a man to that villa, I had died in their arms at the height of passion. It was only now, as I stood on the terrace of the house overlooking the Mediterranean, that I knew that it was the villa that had drawn me back to the island. I felt stupid; it was so obvious that I should have known it all along. It was fate that I return, not least signaled by the fact that the villa obviously was empty, ready to be occupied once more.

I told myself a dozen times that it was fate that I should take up the strands of my Bellapais villa existence, as I drove down to the house where my landlady, Layla, lived, parked the car on the side of the cobbled lane, and wandered into the courtyard. Two small children were playing in the coolness of the small garden and the girl ran off screaming, "Grandma."

When Layla emerged, I recognized her immediately. So little seemed to have changed in the time I had been gone.

"Ah, Alister," she said smiling "You on holiday?" she asked, "Come in. coffee?" she added, leading the way into the front room of the house. Her eyes were welcoming, but there was no fire in them—either of desire or anger. She had closed that part of her past, and I understood, with only a slight tinge of regret, in an instant that we would not speak of what once was, let alone act on it.

A good-looking man was in there resting his plastered leg up on the sofa in front of him.

"My son," she said. "Baris. Baris Ergun."

"You have a son," I stated, rather nonsensically. I didn't ask how she had acquired this solidly bodied; seemingly half asleep man, who appeared to be somewhere in his mid-to-late twenties. Although surely he must be younger than that, I thought. I knew from the rental papers that Layla's last name now was Turkish—Ergun—but I hadn't been aware of any Turk in the picture when I was fucking her.

"Mr. Taylor has come," Layla said to her son, as if coming back was hardly significant. "I told you of the Australian gentlemen who was living at the villa when we were liberated."

The son, Baris, grunted and sat up on the overstuffed sofa covered in cheap floral cotton. He rubbed his eyes. He was still very presentable, but I could see that, like most Turkish men, he very likely would quickly go to fat or craggy wrinkles— or both—from here.

"You are lucky the villa is free again," Layla was saying. "We now mostly rent to holiday people, for a month. They all want to come and soak up the atmosphere of where the *Alexandria Quartet* was written, but only for a month at a time," she added as if it was an insult to be expected to let it out for so short a time.

I nearly laughed at that image. I wondered how pleased they would be to have known the atmosphere of my own—and Layla's as well—sensual habitation there that had overlain Durrell's residency.

"I am working here for six months," I said, "A trial."

"You will stay," she replied, and I noticed the son look at her with a frown.

"Maybe," I said, "I have to see. Things have changed."

"Nothing has changed," Layla said emphatically. "This is still the best place for you. For a time, there was another young man, a Canadian, there in the villa who reminded me so much of you. I thought that he would stay as well. But there were rumors. And eventually he left. Just like you did. I had wanted him to take Baris with him, to help Baris make his way in the greater world. But he just left. Like you, he just left."

I felt at a loss for words. I wondered how much she knew about my life beyond our trysts in the villa—just how much the young Turkish Cypriot men had talked about me. And I wondered what Layla meant about this Canadian being like me. She obviously had been fond of him; I could tell it in her smile when she spoke of him. The same smile she graced me with. And why the reference to Baris?

We drank strong Turkish coffee in small cups and ate Turkish delight as the son talked sporadically to me of the new developments in the Turkish-controlled portion of the island, and she disappeared into the kitchen, leaving him to appear to make the arrangements. He seemed hesitant.

But my life seemed to unfold without my conscious thought, and I got back into my hire car, knowing that when it was cleaned, I was taking the villa again.

My work was the same but different, and the staff in the office were more modern in some ways. And there were more European faces on the street than I had expected. The new apartments appearing everywhere on the slopes were mainly full of English people, with a smattering of other Europeans. The less affluent, or more optimistic, forced out of the other half of Cyprus by the high prices and taking a chance that Turkish Cyprus would stay stable, willing to take the chance because it was dirt cheap in comparison.

I stayed in a hotel until the villa was ready, finding that there was little suitable accommodation in the harbor town of Kyrenia and that being in the smaller mountainside village of Bellapais was probably convenient while I worked out my six-month trial.

In a week I was already back into the life of the village as if I had never gone. Then my manager suddenly resigned his post to take his wife home to America for treatment of some cancer that had been found late, and I was told I'd be filling in for him. Everything seemed to be conspiring to ensure I stayed there, as I knew his job was mine if I did.

After I got the news, I went back to the hotel and stripped off and looked at myself in the mirror, knowing what my real fear was. I was in good firm shape, but I had been twenty-five back then when I had first left. Now I was nearly sixty. In Australia I had cruised the places where Mediterranean men had congregated. The mild Greeks escaping from their small islands, or born in Melbourne, and the Turks, Lebanese, Palestinians, refugees from half a dozen civil wars. And then in time I had ogled their descendants. Young Australians of Mediterranean descent, men with the beauty and grace of cats. And occasionally they had ended up with me and found me more than satisfactory. And sometimes I had paid them in one way or another. But in the last years, it had been their fathers and uncles who had fucked me most.

I looked in the mirror and knew what really frightened me. That I would go down from my villa to the café on the square and would return alone too often.

I moved just the bare necessities into the villa, saying to myself that I was only trialing it. That the drive might be too much each day. But really wanting to be free to leave quickly without a fuss, if I couldn't bear to stay. And I was nervous. More than I had been for years.

The first day I was half hard knowing that that night I would be going down to the square and into the café and sitting on a stool by the bar and eyeing them off. And I was afraid, afraid of being the desperate old gay man sitting there like he was begging.

I went down to the square in the twilight after dinner, and the fairy lights in the olive trees around the fringe of the café's stone terrace were there still. And in that soft light I could hear the achingly familiar twittering laughter of the Mediterranean men and see the wisps of strong Turkish tobacco smoke drifting up into the night.

I walked into the café and took a stool by the bar, ordering a beer from the wiry waiter who brought it to me ice cold and refreshing. I nervously eyed the men about me and a few looked at me briefly, but I saw the young men of the type I had once adored and been eyed off by laughing together and ignoring me. Then one turned and looked my way, and I thought I saw that look start, before a friend gripped his shoulder and he turned away.

"You used to come here," a voice said behind me, and I turned to find the waiter smiling at me shyly. "Many years ago," he added.

"Yes," I replied, glad of something to break the tension in the air. "Nearly thirty years ago." And I realized the face was familiar. "Mustafa," I said, amazed "You were here then."

He nodded shyly. He was no longer lean and wiry as he had been, but, by and large, he was holding his age well, and I remembered that he had come to the villa with me more than once and had fucked me long and hard.

"You are back at the villa?" he asked

"Yes," I replied.

"I am off at ten. Maybe I come see you there. Remember old times," he said, and I smiled at him, reassured that tonight at least would be familiar.

I stayed till the café closed, and we walked up the cobbled lane together, saying little.

In the villa, he playfully pushed me back to the wall inside the door and squeezed my package, then followed me as I removed my clothes and led the way to the bedroom. I hadn't dared to get a lounger for the patio. Knowing there would be nothing worse than to have it there and never use it. To see it every day, accusing me of being too old and a fool to imagine I could recapture the past.

So, instead, Mustafa pushed me onto my bed and I stripped my briefs off as I lay back. My cock was hard and dripping as he pulled off his own pants and briefs and I looked at the body of a man who worked hard—solidly built, with ropey muscle across his belly. His tool was surprisingly thick for a man of such advanced age, and I remembered it had surprised me when I was young. As my own large piece had surprised him.

I lay back, and he was casual and experienced as he opened me up with his calloused fingers and then entered me. My channel opened suddenly for him and pulled him in, playing a long remembered game. He fucked me deep and hard with obvious eagerness, and I lay back and moved my hips with him and moaned, happy to be there, more than happy for it to be just as it was, a familiar friendly fuck. But also a good hard one. And I spouted up my belly quickly as the tension drained from me and I moaned and moved in tune with him. With his pumping hips and driving tool. He came, and laughed a shy little laugh of satisfaction and pleasure and leant over me as if to kiss me. And he did. A big friendly kiss.

I was busy until the weekend, when I wandered down to the café on the square after lunch and took a chair at a small table by the door and sat there in the warmth of autumn, ogling the local Turkish Cypriot men and feeling the reassuring pleasure

80

of several of them ogling me. Mostly older men, and some starting to spread from too much time spent sitting idly in the café. But when I returned to my villa, it was with a man who had still not lost the last shadow of the beauty of his youth, and he was rough and demanding as he took me. The sort of man I wanted. That I needed. The dark olive-skinned body, with its heavy splashes of glossy, curly, black hair over his chest and belly overpowering me. Fucking me hard and deep and for so long that he seemed to have been saving himself just for me.

I may not have recaptured the past completely, but I knew that the last few weeks had been my journey home, and that I had arrived at last.

On Monday morning I drove into the city and parked at my office, where I quickly made some excuse and left, going in search of a lounger for the terrace of my villa.

I thought my journey had ended, that I had finally found a place to grow old and to continue the sensual pleasures I had sought in life. But I was wrong. As it turned out, It didn't even stay the six months I had originally planned.

One evening when I drifted down to the Tree of Idleness café in the Bellapais square in search of a man to satisfy me for the night, I happened to find a half-drunk Baris there. Baris, Layla's son. He took note of me immediately, and he gave me that look, the look I had grown to know signaled someone willing to climb the cobble-stoned street back up to my villa with me.

Baris was a strong and forceful lover, and even though, not yet thirty, he had seemed to be tottering on the edge of spent in the world of Turkish men, he was still virile and long lasting. We had barely entered the door into the entryway of the villa than he was pushing me to my knees and opening his trousers. I gave him suck as he controlled my head with his fists buried tightly in my hair. He had all that he needed with him, and I was quickly down on all fours on the wool rug at the entry, the split foil of a condom packet had landed on the stone floor beside me, and he was opening my channel up with lubed fingers.

He fucked me like a dog, crouched over me, his thighs straddling my hips. He rode me hard and deep and with anger, answering every one of my pleas for relief with a long, strong thrust inside me. And I loved it. When I had come, I collapsed on the floor and he stood up, looming over me, panting, and not yet satisfied.

"Get up," he commanded.

"Sorry," I muttered, as I struggled to my feet. "I know you haven't . . . here the bedroom's through—"

"I know where the fuckin' bedroom is," He said. "I've been here before."

And he did know where it was. He grabbed me by the arm and propelled me into the bedroom and onto my back on the bed. I was naked, but he still had his trousers around his calves and his shirt on his back, but open and unbuttoned. He stripped off the trousers and shirt and stood there, panting heavily in front of me.

I had been wrong. He was still beautiful. Well formed, tightly muscled, hard belly heaving in his need and lust and angry intent. And then I gasped. That was not all he was. He was the spitting image of me thirty-five years ago. Realization flooded in—but too late.

He pounced on me, grabbing my calves and forcing them wide apart, and insinuating his hips between my thighs and, lifting my pelvis off the bed with the power in his grip, thrust deep inside me with one long slide.

"No, Baris," I cried out. "You can't . . . we can't."

But then he dropped one of my thighs and backhanded me across the mouth into silence as I succumbed in sobs and moans and grunts and sighs, as Baris showed that he most definitely could. That we could. That, in my shame, even knowing what I knew now, I could melt to him and move my hips with his plowing and come again when he came.

He left me, alone, in the bedroom of the Bellapais villa, as quickly and quietly and without another word as he had thrown me to the floor and doggy fucked me as soon as we had entered the villa.

The next morning, in trepidation, having no idea what to say, I took the drive down the long, winding, graveled road from Bellapais into the harbor town of Kyrenia—to Layla's house.

She only half-way opened the door to me. No Baris was not home. Baris had gone away. She had sent him away. And, no, she wouldn't tell me where he was. Nor was there anything she wanted to hear from me. She wasn't angry or even resentful. Just sad, very sad.

I left the island that day. And I don't plan to return again.

Chapter 7: Kessel Possession

by habu

I lived and worked in Cyprus as a cultural affairs officer at the American embassy in the mid 1980s, and while living there, I developed quite a taste for young Turkish men. If you could get a good-looking, well-constructed Turkish guy before he got too far into his forties, you could almost guarantee you'd have something forceful, vigorous, straightforward, and good natured to play with. You also, quite often, would have a guy with a pretty heavy pelt on him. Now, I didn't particularly favor a hairy guy in general, but on a Turk, it could be quite arousing, and sometimes I just felt like rubbing my nipples against a fine chest of hair.

I was young then, though, and hadn't quite accepted the reality that I liked men as well as I liked women. I latched into that reality in a subsequent posting to Southeast Asia, and with that realization flowed in thoughts of loss at what I had missed when I was in Cyprus the first time. So, I jumped at another Cyprus assignment as soon as one was available.

When I returned to the island in the mid 1990s, this time in charge of the embassy's cultural program, it still was a divided island, with the southern two thirds being in Greek hands and the northern, more isolated, third in Turkish hands, with a UN-guarded "Green" zone separating the two belligerent sides. I was able to go back and forth between the sides with my job and, now with my new appreciation of men, I could see that both Greek and Turkish young men had their good points.

I quickly found, though, that the Turks—at least the Turkish Cypriots—had fewer inhibitions against male-male activity than the Greek Cypriots did as a rule, despite the historical reputation of the Greeks, although it was never difficult to make a hookup of either. The Turkish men were just more matter of fact and lusty in their fucking and weren't given to long drawn-out preliminaries if they saw something they were interested in.

Fortuitously, my position entailed working and entertaining on both sides of a belligerent border that could be closed down tight for days at a time at a moment's notice, so I was permitted to have a residence on the Turkish side of the island as well as the Greek. Long an admirer of the British writer Lawrence Durrell and his *Alexandria Quartet* and travelogue books, including the classic *Bitter Lemons*, about Cyprus, I had discovered that not only had he written these works while living in a mountainside villa in the medieval abbey village of Bellapais high on the Kyrenia range overlooking the harbor castle town of Kyrenia on the northern coast, but that the villa was for rent when I was looking for a retreat in the Turkish zone.

This was perfect for me. I was writing novels as well, and would, I knew, gain inspiration from doing so in the villa where Durrell penned his masterpieces.

Thus, one fine afternoon I found myself sipping thick Turkish coffee in the dimly lit living room of an ancient, but remarkably well-preserved woman in her Kyrenia house. I had been cried on to Layla Ergun as the keeper of the Durrell flame in northern Cyprus and the landlady for the villa he also once rented in Bellapais. I was almost speechless in meeting the woman, as I had been told that she had been the model for one of Durrell's main characters in the *Quartet*, and I searched my brain while we spoke for clues to which character that was.

While we spoke, a handsome man of thirty or so, identified as her son, Baris, moved quietly around fetching this and that for his mother, who seemed too frail to move from her overstuffed, floral-printed sofa under her own power. Regardless, she looked regal and talked in a clear, steady, strong voice. I couldn't quite decide the origin of her Baris. He had a Turkish name, but he didn't look exactly Turkish to me. But he was quite well turned out, in a dark, well-muscled sort of way. I vaguely found myself wondering if he was heavily hirsute. For some reason that had become a fetish of mine.

But then I supposed there was no particular reason he should look terribly Turkish. Layla wasn't Turkish. If she had figured in Durrell's book, she would be Egyptian and, even then, as much classical Greek as northern African.

After a gentle interrogation, helped along, no doubt, by my writing credentials and intent to pen novels during my stay in the villa, Layla Ergun declared that the villa was, in fact, available for rent and that her son, Baris, could take me up there and show it to me if I was interested.

I was, of course, interested. And from the looks that Baris had been giving me, I determined that he was interested in me too. I seemed to attract men and to signal with little effort my availability. And I usually could tell at a glance when a man wanted me.

I loved the villa. It was exactly what I imagined it would be from reading Durrell. Baris showed me the ground-floor bedroom, with windows opening to the sea on three sides. He showed me the central living area, with three French doors out onto the cliffside terrace and its swimming pool. He showed me the small, but functional kitchen. He showed me the two-bedroom second floor that had been added since Durrell's time. He showed me the native stone terrace overlooking the wide breadth of the Mediterranean, the harbor town of Kyrenia below and the ruins of the Lusignan crusader castle of St. Hilarion brooding on the ridgeline above.

And then he showed me his magnificent, hard cock. And he covered me from behind, his hands holding my wrists, as I gripped the stone wall hard in a wide stance, leaning out over the cliff and watching the ships glide on the blue Mediterranean, as he fucked me deeply and swiftly from behind and nuzzled my neck and whispered into my ear.

"Not only Durrell was inspired to write here," he was whispering. "There was another, Mark Amalfi, whose writing might be more to your liking."

"Amalfi?" I murmured with a groan. "Oh, yes. There, Just like that. Ohhh, god, yes. More to my liking?"

"Yes, he wrote what should have been a classic right here. Want me to recite some of him? I can? You will like it."

"Yes, yes, please. Groannnn. Oh, yes."

Baris's stroking picked up a new rhythm. Still deep, but the cadence set to his recitation.

"Ahh, the days of drifting down to the Tree of Idleness in the square in the late afternoon and sitting ogling the local Turkish Cypriot men and letting them ogle me until I got that certain look from one I fancied. Then taking him up to my rented villa and letting him vigorously, joyously, and noisily fuck my brains out on a lounger under the sun on the terrace overlooking the Mediterranean.

"That would be this terrace," Baris said with a low, hoarse laugh. Do you like being fucked to sounds of the villa, to the life of this place?"

"Oh, yes, yes," I whispered. "Don't stop. Please don't stop."

"Don't stop fucking you or don't stop reciting Amalfi?" Baris asked.

"Both. Don't stop either," I cried out.

Baris took up the cadence of the prose once more:

"And then back down to the square in the twilight after dinner with those fairy lights in the olive trees around the fringe of the stone café terrace, and, in that soft light and twittering laughter of the Mediterranean men and wisps of strong Turkish tobacco drifting up, eyeing and being eyed until I got the certain look from one I fancied and took him back up to the villa and let him fuck me in long, slow, sweeping strokes on the terrace under the stars."

"Oh, god, I think I'm going to come," I cried out.

The recitation continued through my groans and panting.

"And maybe, if he was really, really beautiful and masterful, taking him back to my bed for a night of sleep broken by brief periods of wanton lust, waking to the feel of a hot poker at my hole and a wheedling whisper for permission at my ear and arching back to accept the homage of a throbbing need to be deep inside me. Breakfasting on the terrace by the small pool

88

and then pulling him into the pool and wrapping my legs around his waist and letting the swirling water soften the rhythmic in and outing as I threw my head back and watched the morning Mediterranean light filter through the sighing branches of the olive trees and thought about my late afternoon visit to the Tree of Idleness café in the Bellapais square, already assessing which eyes I would respond to today."

And then I came.

* * * *

In the coming weeks, I found I was spending more and more of my time—all of my weekends—on the Turkish side at the Bellapais villa. Writing by day at the desk in the living room, under a peculiar, but haunting and melancholy oil painting of an unoccupied café table against a sun-drenched ochre-colored wall. And at other times sitting on the terrace and sipping wine and going over program plans for the embassy cultural events on the terrace in the evening, as the sun set behind me below the Kyrenia range ridgeline, lighting up the white and umber walls and red-tiled roofs of the castle harbor town below me. And then, when darkness drifted in, I, in turn, found myself drifting down to the Tree of Idleness café in the Bellapais abbey square and repeating the images that Baris had set in my mind when he was reciting from Amalfi's book and while he was fucking me that first time.

Sometimes Baris would be at the café, and, if he was, he had pride of place, by unspoken right, to come back to the villa with me. He fucked with anger and with complete focus and abandon, and within the first few weeks, he had taken me in every room of the villa. It was almost as if he was trying to leave his dominant mark on the villa, in some sort of struggle with the building itself.

But there were other men, too, and, increasingly I was becoming open about it. So open that the café's owner, Mustafa Ergun, took me aside one evening and warned me that my position with the American embassy was just too high profile and that for my own good, I should look farther a field for my sexual pleasure. And he told me where to look.

It thus unfolded that after a brief Friday-afternoon appearance at the office in the Turkish sector of Nicosia, the capital—which the Turks called Lefkosa, the next week I was racing my BMW convertible across the width of the island to the remote Salamis Bay Hotel. This hotel sat on a rocky beach at the edge of the ancient ruins of the Greek city of Salamis, which had been founded by the Greek troops returning from the sack of Troy and had been destroyed by an earthquake and largely reclaimed by the Mediterranean Sea in the third century BC. I had picked this destination, at Mustafa Ergun's suggestion, because it was in a remote corner of the island, where it was unlikely I'd be recognized, it boasted an infamous nude tourist beach, and Mustafa had given me the address of a small gay bar near the hotel. I wanted to make the most of my free weekend on the Turkish side.

When I got to the eastern end of the island, I got off the not-so-good direct road to Salamis onto the really-not-so-good coastal road so that I could locate the bar I wanted to go to that evening. I found it by following the really bad music of a live band gearing up in the twilight hour before the sun sank below the Troodos Mountains at the other end of the island. It was a beach bar composed of beverage carts surrounded by bar stools under grass umbrellas around an ill-kept swimming pool on a terrace that jutted out over the Mediterranean. The enclosure was barely sectioned off from the view of the road by a scraggly bamboo-slatted fence.

I could see that guys were already arriving for the evening; it looked like a young crowd and mostly the queen type, although I saw some well-cut studs among them. I could see that the typical attire was on the minimalist side. I stopped the BMW at the side of the road near the entrance to the bar to get a better look, and one of the more studly of the youngsters, a lithe, dark-but smooth-skinned guy appearing to be nineteen or twenty whistled and came over to the car. From the way he was looking the car over, I could tell he was whistling at the machine, not at me. But he at least was polite enough to ask me, with a toothy grin and a leer, if I was coming in to the bar, and I told him I might drop back later.

The Salamis Bay Hotel, a seven-story balconied building that would have looked out of place on this desolate coast if it hadn't itself lacked a renovation in two decades, was only about a ten-minute drive from the bar. I stopped in the hotel's lobby bar for an Efes beer to knock away the dust of the road between Lefkosa and the coast and then went up to my seventh-floor suite.

I suppose they called this a suite only because I had my own bathroom; it certainly didn't boast many amenities. But it was fine for my purposes. I'm sure the diplomatic plates on my BMW had something to do with the relative royal treatment I was getting here, although, of course, I registered under a false name. There was a carpet on the floor that didn't look too mildewed, I may have gotten the only queen-sized bed in the hotel, and there was an expansive balcony overlooking the Salamis ruins and that would afford a spectacular view of sunrise over the Mediterranean—if I was awake at sunrise.

With a view to the attire I'd seen entering the gay beach bar, I opted for low-rise cut-offs and sandals, a money clip, a couple of condoms, and my car keys—and nothing else, including briefs. I wasn't here to do much shopping; I was here to get laid.

The music in the bar was still bad when I got there, but it was a whole lot louder than it had been before, and there was a whole lot larger crowd too, swaying to the music, hips close together, or swimming—and, I could tell, fucking—in shadows in the central swimming pool. Cheap strobe lighting was flitting around everywhere, making the patrons frenetically multicolored and helping to mask where they had their hands. I could tell I was making quite a stir in the place as an alluring foreign element, and a path parted between me and one of the bars under the grass umbrellas as I walked in.

I asked for an Efes beer, and my American accent made the whole place my bosom buddy. Within seconds, I had the best of what I could see sniffing around me, looking for an opening. I gave the eye nod to a heavily muscled construction worker type in badly worn jeans and a black muscle T-shirt with a Harley-Davidson logo that must have set him back a week's pay, even though it obviously was a cheap knockoff. He was handsome in an ugly "don't mess with me" sort of way—swarthy of skin, with a two-day's growth of beard, and coarse, curly black hair trying to escape from every opening in his T. Just the change of pace I was in the mood for.

Half way through my Efes, he was sitting on a bar stool, with his legs around my hips and pulling my butt into his hard basket. He was moving my pelvis around on his crotch to the beat of the music, and I could feel that he wanted me in the worst way. Another quite acceptable candidate was trying to get my attention. He was standing close into the front of me. He had a palm of one hand over one of my nipples and took my beer bottle from me with his other hand, poked his tongue into it suggestively, and gave me a lot of "cum hither" eye work. He handed the bottle back to me and was moving his face into mine, probably for a sloppy kiss, when there was a deep-grunted challenge from the guy who was lapping me and a beefy arm came out and pushed the challenger away. The battle for my attention seemed to be over then.

I still hadn't finished my beer when my host snaked his hand around and pushed it under my waistband and held me close to his pushing cock with a skin-on-skin grip on my cock and balls. Then he was unbuttoning and unzipping my cut-offs with his other hand, and I think he would have fucked me right there and then on the bar stool, if I hadn't taken charge and removed his hands and told him that if he wanted to fuck me he'd have to come back to my hotel room. He didn't like that idea, but I started making eye contact with the next best candidates nearby, and he said that, OK, he'd leave the bar with me.

When we got out into the parking lot, the young stud from earlier in the day was sitting on the trunk of my BMW. He looked disappointed when he saw me coming out with another guy—a guy who easily could have snapped him in two. As we were getting in the car, though, I told the young guy I was staying at the Salamis Bay Hotel, and if he wanted to take a ride in my convertible and was in front of the hotel Sunday morning, I might be able to give him one. He seemed quite satisfied with that and waved vigorously as we pulled out of the parking lot.

My "date" asked me to stop the car and let him out before we got to the hotel entrance. He said he was known there and not particularly welcome and would have to come up the back stairs. I gave him my room number and left him there at the side of the road.

He arrived at my room door almost before I did. He had his hands all over me and was starting to wrestle me to the carpet as soon as I let him in the door and shut it. But I told him he would have to both shower thoroughly and use a condom if he wanted to fuck me. This didn't set well with him, but I managed to get him into the bathroom and declined his demand that I come in with him, although I said I'd be taking a shower before we fucked too. I asked him if he'd brought a condom, and he gave me a negative, sinister look. I was to find that the Turkish men wouldn't voluntarily use protection. This guy told me condoms were unmanly while he glowered at me. I told him he'd either have to use one or leave, and I was a little scared he'd just take me there on his own terms. He certainly could have done that, but perhaps whatever trouble he was in with the hotel combined with having to deal with an American, with unknown but highly probable clout, was keeping him in line, if only barely.

After he'd showered, he padded out into the room naked, and I saw that I had picked pretty well. His cock wasn't overly large sized, but it was quite serviceable, and his body was beautifully shaped. As a bonus, the heavy pelting on him was intriguing and gave my cock a little lurch. It was going to be like being fucked by a wild bear. I was game to try that.

I took no chances and locked the bathroom door while I showered and cleaned myself out well. When I came back into the room, expecting to see him stretched out on the bed, the room was empty. Then I saw him, sitting, still naked, out on the balcony, sulking at what he had to do to get some tail. I grabbed and opened a condom packet and picked up a tube of lube and came out on the balcony. He lost his sulk when I dropped my towel and he saw what a good deal he was getting. We engaged in our first kiss, me standing over him, while I rolled the condom on his erect dick and lathered lube over his tool. Then, knowing he wasn't going to put up with further delay, I straddled his thighs, facing him, positioned his cock at my back door, and descended on his manhood. He let out a hissing sound as I sheathed his cock with my channel, and I helped his mouth find one of my nipples.

I slid up and down on his pole for a few minutes, with him making grunting sounds that increased in intensity. I didn't figure that he was going to allow me control for very long like this, and I was right. With a primeval, guttural sound from deep inside him, He stood, briefly losing purchase in my ass with his cock, and carried me into the bedroom, slammed me down on my belly on the bed, got one of my arms in a hammer lock behind my back, forced my legs apart with his knees, positioned his cock at the entrance of my hole with his other hand, and then dove his cock into me. I screamed and nearly arched my body off of the surface of the bed as he tunneled his way up me, pounding me and pounding me, showing me who was the boss. Half way to lift off, he released my arm from his grip, circled his hands under my pelvis, sheathed my cock in one hand and cupped my balls in the other, and fairly lifted my feet off the floor as he pumped me back and forth on his cock.

When we'd both shot off, he fell on top of me and lay there, both of us heaving, until our breathing became regularized. Then he pulled off me, put his clothes back on, gave me a big grin of thanks, and was gone. Honest and straightforward. We'd both gotten what we wanted with a minimum of fuss. I hadn't expected him to stay the night or anything, and the intensity of the fuck had made me just as glad that he didn't stay around to do it again. But my guess was that he really didn't want to be caught in the hotel or inside one of its patrons and was headed back to the beach bar for his next fuck.

I was awake to catch the sunrise on my balcony after all, and a spectacular view it was.

I breakfasted in the hotel dining room, and the food wasn't half bad. While I was eating, I noticed a well-turned waiter giving me the once over more than once, and I almost choked on my coffee when I realized he had been one of my "next best alternatives" in my bar hop of the previous evening. I filed his presence away as a possible chapter in my Turk weekend.

Then it was out to the nude tourist beach. Both Greek and Turkish societies are puritanical, but both are also highly entrepreneurial. There were nude beaches in both sectors of the island, but, by law, they were restricted to the foreign tourists, and the locals supposedly were limited to watching from the far-off fringes with binoculars. This being the Mediterranean, however, a local could get onto the beach just by paying off the police who were there to keep them away and also to see that there was no actual, graphic sex acts being performed on the beach. Heavy petting didn't seem to violate this law, but maybe the police guards on duty just considered permitting that to be a fringe benefit for themselves. In another anomaly of the Greek and Turkish systems on this, woman nude tourists were just to be ogled, on pain of serious punishment, but nude men tourists were accepted as advertising their availability.

Thus it was that when I arrived at the beach and set out my towel and then stripped off my skimpy Speedo—the same size Speedo I had used for months to build up a very nice tan—what was left untanned became pretty much a billboard, and a nice enough advertisement that I was surrounded by men of several different nationalities in no time flat. This was to be a Turk weekend, though, so I waved off the Scandinavians and Israelis and concentrated on the Turkish possibilities. Several of these men looked like they would do, and I tried a few out with some hands work—theirs on me and mine on them—an activity they didn't seem to mind sharing—and the local police didn't mind watching. Four young men seemed to arouse me sufficiently, and when I'd brought up the condom requirement and asked if they had come prepared, I was down to two.

Rather than make choices between these two, when I couldn't really tell much of a difference between them except that one had a slightly bigger cock than the other, I just named them Turk A (nice cock) and Turk B (nicer cock) and asked what we were to do about the no sex on the beach rule and the roving police. They both laughed, gathered up a large beach towel and me, and hustled me down to the water. We entered the water and moved around a rock formation, where there was a little cover surrounded by smooth rocks, a place that could not be seen from the beach.

Turk A stretched his towel out on one of these rocks, and the three of us loosened each other up with several minutes of mutual admiration of body parts and stroking and sucking of same, accompanied by much kissing and good-natured laughing. At length, Turk A pushed me on my back on the towel and I opened my legs wide for him and let him prepare my asshole for his onslaught. I made sure he was sheathed by rolling a condom on him myself, and then Turk B stretched out beside me and played with my nipples and cock and balls while Turk A fucked me as vigorously as my "date" from the previous evening had. When both he and I had come, I rolled a condom onto Turk B and, at his direction, waded out into the water with him. When we were standing in water nearly up to our nipples, I climbed his torso in the buoyant water, wrapping my legs around his waist and helping him to insert his nicer cock in my ass, and he fucked up into me there in the turquoise-blue, calm Mediterranean.

When we returned to the beach, I was exhausted enough from the attention from those two Turks that I pulled my Speedo back on and just lay baking in the sun, fully satisfied with how my weekend was going.

Before the afternoon was over I found out why the local police were so forgiving of sexual activity on the beach. I was still being propositioned by a bevy of young guys when a policeman came up to us. The guys scattered and I thought maybe I'd be given some grief, but the cop, another young, highly presentable Turk, simply smiled shyly at me and told me what he'd like to do and showed me that he'd even brought his own condom. I didn't want to get in the bad graces of anyone in authority, and he really was quite nice looking and polite, so I let him lead me over to a shed where the beach protectors went to get out of the sun, and he fucked me from behind up against the wall, making very pleased sounds through the whole coupling.

When I entered the hotel from my jaunt on the beach, the "another nice candidate" hotel employee was waiting for me in the lobby. He hailed me as I was crossing to the elevator and asked me, in a very pointed tone, if there was anything he could do to make my stay more comfortable or memorable. I told him I was on my way to my room to take a shower and told him that if he was a masseur or knew of one, sure, I could use a little work on my muscles. While I was showering, he used his pass key and joined me under the spray. Taking my offhand remark to heart, he did a little work on the muscle between my legs there, and then brought me out to the bed, laid me on my belly, and started massaging my shoulder muscles. This only lasted for about twenty seconds before we were rolling around on the bed together and arrived in a sixty-nine position, where we slowly sucked each other off. Then we rolled around some more, and when he'd reloaded, he straddled my hips from behind, his hands holding my arms down on the surface of the bed, and fucked me with what I was learning was typical Turk vigor and enthusiasm and with what I'm sure was the longest cock I took that weekend.

He at least stayed around long enough after the main event for me to run my hands through a Turkish pelt, from chest to pubes. At my invitation, he came back and had me for dessert after I'd eaten dinner in the hotel dining room and slept half the night with me in my hotel bed, proving several times in the night that a Turk can be tender and forceful at the same time.

Sunday morning I had set aside to explore the ruins at Salamis, but when I walked out of the entrance of the hotel, there sat the grinning young Turk I had encountered two days previously at the gay beach bar entrance. He was sitting on the trunk of my car, in expectation of that ride I had promised him. So, I decided to explore him before exploring the ruins and took him for a long ride in the BMW with the top down, stopping and lingering in a little copse of trees well off the road at the edge of the Mediterranean, where I then took him into the backseat of my car and rode him to exhaustion. I had a bigger and longer dick than any I'd seen on a Turk that weekend, and he squealed with delight as I split him asunder and found out that Turks were as good at receiving as giving.

* * * *

Mustafa had been right. I could live the auxiliary life I wanted to live on Cyprus so much more freely in the isolated area of Salamis than near Kyrenia, which was so close to Nicosia that the entire diplomatic community used it as a playground.

And, strangely enough, the villa wasn't much of a writing inspiration for me. Whenever I was there, it was like the walls were whispering me, singing a siren call through the memorable words of Mark Amalfi, calling me to leave my writing and drift down to the Tree of Idleness and bring a young, virile man back with me. I began fantasizing that it was the villa that wanted these young men, more than me. That the villa itself had some sort of voyeuristic need to watch a succession of residents be fucked by the young Turkish studs of the village. And, for some reason, that forlorn oil painting over the desk made me nervous. I felt like it was watching me and judging the casual sexual lifestyle I had fallen into in the Turkish zone.

When the six-month lease was up on the villa, I exchanged it for a large flat in the Turkish sector of Nicosia. This location made much more sense for my programming and it was on the road to Salamis.

In my last visit to Layla Ergun in Kyrenia, I could tell that she was greatly disappointed in my decision not to remain. I picked a day to visit her when I knew Baris wouldn't be there. He wouldn't be there, I knew, because I had arranged an American Cultural Center concert for him to play the baglama— he and Mustafa—the two of them having been among the few who were keeping the old Turkish musical folk traditions alive.

I didn't want Baris to be there. He had become excessively possessive. And he had somehow merged with the villa in my mind. He wanted to fuck me hard and cruelly, within the watching walls of the villa whenever he could trap me there. Both he and the villa had become stifling.

But I felt badly for Layla. She seemed to be failing, and I knew before she said anything in that last meeting, that she had some petition to give me on behalf of her son.

I thought she was babbling incoherently when she first broached the subject.

"Please, can you find a position of my Baris at the American embassy? Something that could lead to immigration and a Green Card? He's really Australian, you know. And they know that here, too. They never have accepted him here, the Turks—either my son or me. And I once thought he would be going to Canada. I've given him to so many men in trying to get him to where he belongs—Australia or America, anywhere but here. He's being eaten up here. The island is swallowing him whole, but for some reason he doesn't want to leave here. He's so sad—and so angry with life. Please, isn't there something you can do?"

I didn't understand half of it. And I didn't want to face the horror of the possibility that Layla Ergun knew exactly what would happen when she sent her son to show me the Bellapais villa. But she was so pitiful, so delicate, so needy—and so attached to my literary idol, Durrell, that, out of respect, I promised to do something.

But, of course, I never did.

Chapter 8: Broken Possession

by sabb

"Here. This is it," Jason called out.

Mark, Andrew, and Kyle joined him in front of the old villa in the winding cobble-stoned village street and, dropping their backpacks onto the uneven cobbles, looked up at it as they got their breath back.

"Why do we end up with an old villa half way up a hill that has no car access?" Andrew asked for the third time.

They ignored him, as they all knew that the road closure was a recent and short-term event, because half the lane was dug up for the installation of a water pipe. Mark took the ancient key from his pocket and, after fiddling, opened one of the pair of big old timber doors that let them into the courtyard.

"Wow," Kyle exclaimed as they entered.

"Its just like he describes it, only more overgrown," Jason added.

They stood in a group for a moment, four good-looking young blonds, lightly muscled, well tanned, and on holiday, wearing loose T-shirts, brightly colored baggy shorts, and leather sandals. They made a very attractive group and had caused heads to turn their way on their walk up through the town from where they had left their hire car parked.

"It smells." Andrew said loudly. "God, I hope it's got a decent bathroom."

"Comfortable beds," Mark added, as they moved inside the villa's entry and through the large open living area.

In the dim light of the room Mark noticed a large painting hanging over the desk that stood against one wall. It seemed oddly familiar. But he didn't know why, because it was nothing but the picture of two empty café chairs against an ochre-colored wall. He no more than glanced at it as he followed the others out to the terrace and found them looking up at the steep concrete staircase to the upper level. Kyle and Mark climbed up first and explored the two bedrooms and then opened the door onto the veranda that topped the large master bedroom below.

"So this is where their great love affair fell apart," Kyle remarked.

"Yes." Mark replied as he moved in behind Kyle and wrapped his arms around him. "Stunning," he added, as they stood there pressed together and looking out at the view that was spread out below them. Taking in the ruins of the sweep of the vista from Byzantine abbey of Bellapais to the ancient castle harbor town of Kyrenia and the blue Mediterranean beyond.

"Here you are," Andrew said loudly, as he and Jason joined them, "Well, I suppose the view from up here is pretty spectacular. Almost worth the climb. So who's sleeping here?"

"We want the bedroom downstairs, the one with the old iron bed," Mark replied, "That was the only bedroom back then."

"How romantic, or perhaps dangerous, sleeping in their old room, maybe even the same bed. Well, the bathroom looks civilized. So, lets get organized, I can't wait to see if the café really has any talent to offer," Andrew shouted, as he swung himself down the stairs in two leaps.

They picked beds, Kyle and Mark sharing the original bedroom downstairs with its big, old, iron bed, Andrew and Jason dragging their packs up the steep staircase and taking the larger of the two rooms upstairs. And two hours later they had unpacked and showered off the heat and the sweat of the climb up from the village square and had congregated in the chairs on the upper veranda.

Kyle made coffee and took it up the stairs to them, and the four young friends sat there, taking in the view of the evening and the light of the setting sun casting shimmering colors over the ocean that lay beyond the ruins, while they drank it.

"So, read us what your uncle wrote back then," Andrew demanded. "The fateful paragraphs that ended it all."

"They didn't end it all," Mark replied, irritated. "There were obviously other issues; they didn't both want the same thing."

"We know that, but that's why he wrote them subconsciously, wasn't it? Because he wanted to have a different life and couldn't be that person Val Cramner wanted him to be?" Jason said quietly, looking intently at Mark.

Mark picked up the book he had in his lap and opened it at a turned over page and read aloud.

Ahh, the days of drifting down to the Tree of Idleness in the square in the late afternoon and sitting ogling the local Turkish Cypriot men and letting them ogle me until I got that certain look from one I fancied. Then taking him up to my rented villa and letting him vigorously, joyously, and noisily fuck my brains out on a lounger under the sun on the terrace overlooking the Mediterranean.

"The loungers are gone," Andrew said, in mock horror. "We've been cheated. I want to fuck on a lounger."

"There is an old one downstairs in the courtyard," Kyle replied, "If you want to bring it up here, go ahead. Now shut up. This is serious."

Mark resumed his reading.

And then back down to the square in the twilight after dinner with those fairy lights in the olive trees around the fringe of the stone café terrace, and, in that soft light and twittering laughter of the Mediterranean men and wisps of strong Turkish tobacco drifting up, eyeing and being eyed until I got the certain look from one I fancied and took him back up to the villa and let him fuck me in long, slow, sweeping strokes on the terrace under the stars.

And maybe, if he was really, really beautiful and masterful, taking him back to my bed for a night of sleep broken by brief periods of wanton lust, waking to the feel of a hot poker at my hole and a wheedling whisper for permission at my ear and arching back to accept the homage of a throbbing need to be deep inside me. Breakfasting on the terrace by the small pool and then pulling him into the pool and wrapping my legs around his waist and letting the swirling water soften the rhythmic in and outing as I threw my head back and watched the morning Mediterranean light filter through the sighing branches of the olive trees and thought about my late afternoon visit to the Tree of Idleness café in the Bellapais square, already assessing which eyes I would respond to today.

There was a few moments silence. Mark was having difficulty not crying.

"We met your uncle, but what was Val like? The man he gave up so he could have the men at the café," Jason asked.

Mark shrugged, tears now on his face, "I saw a photo, and he was very Bohemian looking. Long, curly, light-brown hair. Very slim. And, no jeans, ordinary pants--but with a gauzy white shirt. It made him look slightly androgynous. When I saw him a couple of years ago at the Cramner Art Festival, he was still thin and quite a good-looking old man. Very polite, very proper."

"Not my type," said Andrew airily. "And I'm surprised he was your uncle's type."

"Now?" Jason asked, looking angrily at Andrew and changing the subject.

"I suppose so," Mark replied wiping his eyes. "I suppose it's time."

They left the old villa and descended the steep lane to the square like a flock of beautiful birds migrating in pursuit of the sun, and heads turned, and admiring looks followed them.

At the square they wandered over to the old tree that dominated it, now lit up with fairy lights in the early twilight, and saw the tables beneath it starting to fill up. Mostly with local Turkish Cypriot men, but with a smattering of pale tourists also.

Then the four visitors moved on and crossed the road to the forecourt of the ruins of the old Bellapais Abbey, with it's curved stone doorways and thin, tall funeral cypress trees, and stopped, forming a half circle around Mark.

"Now, Mark," Kyle said. "Now's the time."

Mark pulled a sheet of paper out of the bag he'd carried down from the villa and read. "My uncle, the novelist, Mark Amalfi, first came to Cyprus in 1962. He came with his . . . lover, Lord Valery Cramner, to escape the scandal they had caused in England and find somewhere they could be together. But things didn't work out between them."

The young Mark paused and sniffed, feeling embarrassed that he was teary in front of this friends, and also strangers, as people were looking at them now. Obviously wondering what they were doing.

"On that first visit, Mark fell in love with Durrell's villa and the village of Bellapais. Here he found himself—and who he really was—and here his writing matured and he wrote some of his finest novels. Mark returned to this village several times over the years, and each time he came he wrote some of his best work. Before he died, he allowed me to read the story of his first time here and said that he hoped it would help me to understand why it was his wish to have his ashes scattered here. And he asked me if I would do that for him."

Mark choked on the last words. He looked up, trying to look in control of himself, though tears were now running down his cheeks. "That is why we are here today. As my uncle requested, I am here to scatter his ashes where he wanted them to be scattered."

Mark folded the paper up and slipped it back inside the overnight bag he had carried down from the villa. Then he pulled a cardboard box from the bag and returning to the wall separating the path from the abbey garden, rampant with wild flowers, he fumbled open the lid of the box and began to walk along the wall, letting the ashes it contained trickle out slowly into the twilight darkness and scatter on the evening breeze to eventually fall in the cascade of flowers below or rise up and settle among the leaves of the trees around the square. When the box was empty, Mark stood still for a while, remembering the man he had both admired and felt sorry for, before turning to gaze at the square and the twinkling fairy lights and the laughing, talking men gathered there in the glow of the lights set up among the trees.

"He described it so well in his memoirs," he said to Kyle, who had joined him.

"And you did well," Kyle told him, putting an arm around Mark and giving his lover a gentle kiss on the lips. "Now, lets eat, I'm starving."

The next day the group took the hire car and made an excursion to Seven Mile beach, the center of the 1974 invasion of the island by Turkish forces, and when they returned in the afternoon, they parked the car as near to the square as they could and headed to the café again. They were recognized from the evening before, when they had eaten there after the scattering of the ashes, and while they ate, three young local men joined them and practiced their English with them, before suddenly saying they had to return to work and hurrying off.

The walk back up to the villa was taken slowly, and once they arrived, they separated and headed to their rooms, collapsing on the beds in the cool house and escaping the heat of the afternoon.

"Do you think this place really has some pull on the men who stay here? The men at the café . . . do have something . . . something appealing about them. You've read what my uncle wrote about the way this house seemed to be whispering to him to . . . join them, whatever." Mark asked, trailing off uncertainly.

"No idea," Kyle replied firmly. "I don't hear any whisperings yet, do you? Stop worrying about it. I think they had other problems, Mark. We're fine," he added, rolling on top of Mark and placing his lips against his lover's smooth neck and sucking and nibbling it.

"We're very fine," he added as he pushed Mark's shorts down and took his cock in his hand and stoked it to stiffness as they kissed gently.

Mark's hands slid under Kyle's T and stripped it off him, so his mouth could go to licking at the hair that curled over his lover's chest and suck at the muscles of his shoulders and nuzzle at his arm pits. He loved the sweet smell of Kyle's fresh sweat, and in the heat of the island summer and after their swim in the Mediterranean, he tasted salty as well as fresh.

"Hmmm," he sighed as Kyle moved down the big old iron bed until his mouth found Mark's rod and his body twisted about so that they could sixty-nine, Mark fingering Kyle's ass as he sucked on his dick and cupped his balls. Holding off his own ejaculation, he suddenly rose into a crouch, with his thighs spread wide, and pulled Kyle's butt into his lap but leaving his chest resting on the bed. Then Mark held his cock down as he worked it into his partner's hole.

"Yes, yes," Kyle moaned, widening his stance and moving his butt in time with Mark's thrusts, so that they came together, before collapsing and sleeping.

That evening they all went to the Tree of Idleness café in the square, where they ate traditional island food and ordered cold Efes beers and drank them from the brown bottles. The three young men from the afternoon joined them again, and the visitors switched to a wine the locals recommended and called Cankaya, though the young men stuck to their Efes beers.

"Not bad," Jason said to the tallest of the young men, while sipping his wine and looking into the man's dark eyes over the top of his glass.

"Very good wine. All Turkish wines are very good," the young man replied, smiling broadly.

Jason flirted with him as they argued about the quality of the wine. Andrew had already turned his eyes to the other two young men, their darkness making an attractive contrast to the golden tans and blond hair of the visitors.

Then Jason was standing up and bending over Mark. "I'm heading back," he said. "I am feeling the pull, oooohhh," he added, joking, "And I need the key. I'll leave the doors unlocked."

Mark handed over the ancient key, and Jason and the tall young man disappeared up the cobbled laneway leading to the villa. Andrew hardly seemed to notice, which wasn't really a surprise to Mark or Kyle.

And it wasn't long till the other three men went off also, Andrew claiming he'd show the two local Turkish Cypriots what the villa was like inside.

Kyle smiled after the departing figures. "Well, maybe your uncle knew what he was talking about after all," he joked. "Those two have certainly got 'that certain look' tonight."

"Mmmm," Mark murmured vaguely, his eyes seeming to be wandering over the variety of men seated about them, laughing and smoking in the still air.

Kyle folded an arm around Mark's shoulders, "We'd better give them a bit of time before we head back," he said. "Another drink?"

"Sure," Mark replied, turning a broad smile to him. "Thanks."

The next morning Kyle woke up alone. He'd found it hard to get to sleep the previous night with the loud cries and laughs and moans of the fucking that was going on, coming from upstairs. And the young Turkish Cypriots had left noisily some time in the early hours, waking him again. So he was still tired. But horny too, and he was disappointed when his arm found the other side of the bed empty.

He crawled out of bed and found Mark upstairs on the veranda with his uncle's memoirs open before him, and he leant over his shoulder to see what he was reading

One paragraph jumped out clearly, like an omen.

"I had gone there, to the village café, once, quite innocently. But I had found myself ogling those laughing, muscular, hirsute Turkish men, with their easy, open enjoyment of life and their jovial camaraderie, their dusky skin and flashing eyes and curly black hair."

Mark closed the book quickly and Kyle shook his head to clear the image, but he instinctively grasped the book from Mark's lap and hid it behind his own back, pretending he was playing.

"I was looking for you in bed, and you were gone," he told him, pouting. Then nuzzling Mark's neck and saying, "Come back and I'll make it worth your while."

Mark laughed at him, but he led the way back down. and pushed Kyle back onto the bed. But then he took the time to rescue the book and put it in a drawer of the old chest that stood beside the bed before he went any further. Kyle grabbed him when he turned back, and they made rough, fast love. This time Kyle taking Mark, fucking into him with little preparation, wanting to make him cry out as he rode him, biting his shoulders, marking him, filling him.

Afterwards Kyle said, "Don't get obsessed with that book, Mark—with what happened."

"I'm not," Mark replied guiltily. "But perhaps it's true," he added, turning to his partner. "I could feel something in the café last night. I don't know what it was, but it was there. The pull of the atmosphere in the square, and the men. Don't they appeal to you too?"

Kyle shrugged, "Not really."

The four friends spent the next day roaming the old town of Kyrenia, eating in a small tourist restaurant by the water before exploring the harbor castle ruins—a Byzantine castle inside a Lusignan fortress. Jason and Andrew left the other two there.

"I hear the afternoon call of the café. Ooooh ooooohh," Andrew joked as the pair headed off, half running, over the rough ground of the ruin.

When Mark and he had had enough, Kyle insisted they go back to the villa to eat, and they bought olives and bread, a bottle of the Cankaya wine, and cheese from the small shop behind the square and, hand in hand, carried it up the cobbled lane. They set the food out on the table in the courtyard and had barely finished their meal when the others returned, their arrival signaled by the sound of male low laughter and low voices. Jason and Andrew were each arm in arm with a dark-haired muscular man, not the young men of the night before but other young men, smiling and with flashing eyes. They seemed to burst into the courtyard like a flash flood, sweeping everyone before them. Including Kyle and Mark, who couldn't help returning their smiles and watching them as they moved fluidly into the villa.

"No sleep tonight either," Kyle remarked casually.

But his remark was made more to cover what frightened him, which was that he had lied to Mark and he could feel the pull of the laughter, the dark eyes, easy masculinity and exotic darkness of the young Turkish Cypriot men. The way they moved, their easy grace. He pulled himself up and tried to put them out of his mind.

Mark was silent, looking after the departed men, and Kyle felt a stab of fear.

"He always regretted losing Val," Mark said, turning back and looking intently at Kyle. "My uncle told me he could have been happy with Val and could still have managed occasional opportunities for having other men. He never had another serious relationship, and he said he was happy with that too. But he was so lonely, Kyle. Those last years when he was old and had trouble getting around. And when he came back here the last time, he had to pay or he would leave the café alone; they all knew he'd give them something, and still he sometimes left alone. He said he didn't mind, but he stopped writing anything good, and then he never came to Bellapais again. He seemed to give up on life after that."

"OK." Kyle shrugged irritably, "And Val has been with his partner now for thirty years and is the grand old man of English painting and the arts. That doesn't mean that your uncle and Val would have lasted. And Val probably wouldn't have inherited Cramner House if he hadn't returned to England alone, and there wouldn't be any mecca for young artists and writers."

"You're right, of course. They were exiles here."

"And if there was a pull, well, why didn't Val feel it too?" Kyle asked reasonably.

"Maybe he did. Maybe he just was strong enough and knew what he wanted enough, to resist it."

Kyle looked at him, "Maybe. And maybe there just isn't really any strange force this villa exerts on its occupants. Maybe its just liking to see dark, hairy, good-looking, easy-going men who aren't angsting over what they want for a change, that appeals."

Mark shrugged and didn't add anything, but said unexpectedly, "I was looking at that picture that's hanging over the desk in the living area and I think it was painted by Val. But why would he have painted a picture of two empty chairs? He was always a portraitist."

"I have no idea," Kyle replied, surprised that such a valuable painting should have been hanging in a rental villa in Turkish Cyprus, but knowing Mark knew enough to tell one of Lord Cramner's paintings if he saw it,

They went to bed with the sounds of lusty sex going on above them. And Mark was aroused by it as much as Kyle, and soon they were making their own cries and moans and drowning out those coming from the upper floor.

In the night Mark awoke, needing a piss. He eased himself out of the bed, leaving Kyle sleeping soundly, and padded across the floor naked and barefooted in the dark and let himself out into the villa's entry space, where some light filtered down from upstairs and through the open doors leading from the living room to the courtyard. Upstairs it was quiet, and he vaguely wondered if the local men had gone.

When he'd finished in the bathroom, Mark walked into the kitchen looking for a drink, only to discover in the moonlight coming through the window that one of the young Turkish Cypriot men was already in there, leaning back against the cupboards, drinking Efes straight from the bottle and stoking himself.

The stranger lowered the bottle and set it down on the counter behind him, then reached his arms out invitingly, his thick cock luminous in the moonlight, and bouncing up when he released it. His balls were almost invisible, just hinted at, in the black shadow that indicated where his thighs met.

Mark hesitated, seeing the invitation and feeling and smelling the heat in the room, but holding back, his own cock jumping and moving, but his brain undecided. The image of Kyle in bed washed over him. But then there was something unreal about the scene, and his mind let go, pretending it was a dream. In dreams it was OK to do anything. In dreams there was no logic and no future. Dreams could always be woken up from.

His body moved forward to the young Turk, his eyes roaming over the dim figure, seeing the dark shadows cast by well-used muscles and dark curly hair. When he was only a couple of steps away, the stranger moved forward. His calloused rough hands curled about Mark's waist and turned him, and pushed him forward, till his thighs hit the edge of the rough pine table that stood in the center of the kitchen.

Mark let out a moan as it came to him that this dream was going to be a dream about being taken wildly and roughly. A

111

dream where lust and being wanted and being taken were all that mattered. Were what justified everything.

A rough hand moved between his shoulder blades and pushed him over, onto the table.

Then his head was turned to the side facing the door to the living area, and his cheek rested on the rough wood, and he felt its coolness on his face as he felt the heat of the hand in the center of his back and the Turk's body behind him. And it was no longer a dream. Then he felt fingers, hot, rough, calloused fingers, digging. The calluses rough against his rim as they entered him. He moaned again, seeing himself as a soft cool body being ignited into a throbbing moaning passionate fire by another body, one made for heat. His fingers scrabbled against the rough wood, wanting to grip something so he could lift his head and hump his hips against the fingers entering and working his ass.

Then another figure appeared, weaving about in his field of vision, and there was a low laugh, a free uninhibited one, and a swagger, and the new arrival was on the other side of the table, gripping Mark's hair and pulling his face up and guiding a meaty half hard dick to his mouth.

Behind Mark, hot fingers were slick and pulling out of him, then his butt cheeks were pulled apart roughly, and he felt a hard pole pressing at his rim. It entered him behind as he felt the other cock pushed into his throat, and he gagged.

Soon, one cock was plunging into his guts as another was plunging into his throat, and the two young Turkish Cypriots were gasping and grunting and making remarks as they worked in unison. Plunge, withdraw, plunge, withdraw, twist, sink in and twist, and sink in further. Fucking, fucking, fucking. Their calloused hard-working hands gripped him, at his hips, guiding and holding them, and gripping his head, guiding and holding that.

Mark came, and realized this was what his uncle had discovered at the villa and always yearned for, this wild, free, almost anonymous fucking. Then his mouth was filled with the cum of one young man and the other pulled out of his ass and shot up over his back. The cum falling hot on his flesh. Soon he felt the Turk behind him move away and the one in front pulled out of his mouth and dropped his head, and for a moment he closed his eyes and let his cheek rest against the cool smooth timber of the tabletop as he swam in their semen.

Then he eased himself up till he was standing. The kitchen was empty as if no one had ever been there, but he heard the sound of feet on the stairs and low laughter. Still, if he hadn't had the taste of cum in his mouth and a sore ass Mark could perhaps have believed it had been a dream.

* * * *

Kyle had wanted him. It was that sudden, and that simple. He had gone to the bathroom and left the door open, naturally, and someone had come in behind him just as he finished.

And it had been that sudden. Instinct. Or a force outside himself. He had just stayed there and leant forward and rested his palms flat against the cool concrete wall and arched his back. And the man behind him had accepted the invitation. Had reached around and grasped Kyle's dick as he fisted his own, with Kyle feeling its head brush against his body occasionally as it moved about, getting harder, growing, like his own was under the other hand of his unseen companion.

They made hardly any noise, just grunts, gasps, and cutoff moans, because somehow silence seemed right. No guilt or uncertainty. Kyle wanted it. It was that simple. He had no other thoughts at all.

Then fingers were at his hole, and he arched his back more, pushing his ass toward the fingers, moving his ass about as they entered him. Hard thick fingers, digging, in a hurry. Their owner hot and hard and throbbing and wanting to bury himself inside a warm tight channel. The stranger's hand leaving Kyle's own cock, so he automatically reached down and began slowly stroking himself as the stranger's hand ran over his ass and belly and slid over his body in a brief exploration of the body it was about to enter. Then the cock behind him was pressed to his entrance, and he moaned as he felt how thick and hard it was as it entered him, but with almost no pain. And he wanted it so much. He sighed as it moved past his prostrate and moaned

113

again but didn't come. Then it had bottomed inside him, and he let out a gasp of pure release as he shot his load.

Then he was being fucked slowly at first. Deep and slow, fuuuuck, fuuuuuuck, fuuuuuuck. But that soon became a frenzied pounding that had his legs banging against the toilet seat and his own dick engorging again. The man behind him froze and then jerked several times, and he felt hot cum explode inside him and his own cock stiffen. The man stayed buried in his ass and leant against him breathing hard, Kyle smelling the beer on his breath and his man smell. And the man's arms wrapped around Kyle, his face resting on his back as Kyle supported their combined weight on his one hand against the wall and stroked himself to another ejaculation. Then he collapsed against the cistern, and the man slid off his back and out of Kyle's ass and stood up on his own feet.

Kyle turned and sat down, spent, and in the dim light saw a dark-haired young man, naked and with the curly black hair on his body standing out as an indistinct dark smudge like a fat crucifix set on his torso. Then he had turned, and his pale butt cheeks were big and round and caught the light as he left the bathroom, the undulating of his glutes making Kyle want him again. But then the man disappeared through the door, and Kyle leant back and closed his eyes. He jerked awake and Mark was there standing at the door looking in. And he lay there paralyzed, unable to understand what he had done, but in a moment of panic he realized he was actually lying in bed.

* * * *

The quiet distant laughter and voices of the two young men were calling to Mark, and he followed them in a daze of heat. Going along the passage from the kitchen heading across the living room and out to the steep staircase. But as he passed the desk, something moved in the darkness in the corner of his eye and he turned to look where Val's painting of the two café chairs hung above the desk. In the darkness it looked different, but he didn't stop to see why, the murmuring laughter lured him on. Then he was passing the bedroom door, but as he passed it, he couldn't stop himself from looking in. And in the shadows

114

inside he saw two men fucking on the big old bed, and he stopped, frozen in confusion. A dark man was hunched over a lithe blond on his belly beneath him, the blond writhed and moaned, and the dark man turned his face to Mark.

It was his uncle, Mark Amalfi. Mark had no doubt of it. And the look on his face was one of not just sexual passion and desire, but more of total happiness. A look far beyond any sign of happiness that Mark had ever seen on his uncle's face in life. And he suddenly realized the pale-haired man under Mark, moaning now and moving his hips, was too lean and pale and his hair too long and dark to be Kyle. The young bottom lifted his head and turned it to see the man covering him, and the man above him at that moment reached down and brushed a lock of the curly, shoulder-length, soft-brown hair that fell across his face back. And then he leant down and they kissed a long deep kiss.

In that moment Mark felt his heart and belly fall away inside him, and he almost passed out, as the blood rushed to his head and he closed his eyes. Then as he opened them again, his heart pounding and gasping for air, he saw it was only Kyle lying there on his belly. Alone. There was no one else. Only the familiar solidness of his lover, the muscles of his back highlighted by the shadows. And for a long while Mark clung to the door frame and gasped air in, shivering.

He had never known Kyle mattered so much to him. And it shocked him. Suddenly, he felt overcome with guilt and regret that he had let himself be taken by the two men in the kitchen, risking everything. While Kyle lay there sleeping.

He crawled into the bed, trying not to wake Kyle, easing himself in close behind his lover, cupping his body to him and holding him, knowing he never wanted to lose him.

In his sleep Kyle suddenly threw his arm wide and kicked his legs, waking himself in the gray light of the early morning. Behind him he felt a body and arms around him and he twisted about.

"Oh, Mark," he said in a daze, relieved at seeing who was holding him.

"Yes," Mark said shakily, still awake and holding Kyle tight and kissing his lips. "Did you . . . did you have a bad dream?"

"Yes. Yes a bad dream," Kyle replied, guiltily reaching down and feeling for dried cum on his belly. "I want us to leave here," he added in a rush. "I can feel the power this place has and I want to go. Your uncle was right."

"Yes. Yes, let's go, Kyle," Mark replied quietly. "I'll let the others know," he added, knowing he didn't want Kyle to meet the two young men from the night before, and he was out of the bed and pulling on a pair of boxers before Kyle had taken in his unexpected reply.

"You start packing," he threw over his shoulder as he disappeared through the French doors and into the courtyard. Kyle heard Mark's feet on the stairs as he dragged their backpacks out from under the bed. This morning the house suddenly felt as if it was alive. Alive and angry. And it frightened him. He tried to open the drawers of the old chest, and they stuck and fought him, so that when he had them open at last, he grabbed everything out of them in one go and just threw it into the packs.

Then Mark was back, standing at the door. "They aren't there," he said in a confused and frightened voice. "There's no one upstairs. And Val's painting, there are two men in the chairs now. And I'm sure it's Val and uncle Mark, sitting there looking at each other. We have to leave here," he added, disappearing toward the courtyard. He'd seen Mark's wild untidy packing and not said anything. He could feel it too, the villa seeming to close in on him, grasping at him.

Kyle threw on clothes and grabbed their things from the bathroom.

"Kyle," Mark called and he hurried out to the courtyard to find his partner standing by the closed old doors that let onto the street, and looking down. "Look," he said, pointing.

The big key sat on the paving just inside the doors as if it had been pushed back under them when they were closed.

"Are they locked?" Kyle asked.

Mark stepped forward and pulled them. "Yes. Looks like they went out early. They're locked," he added unnecessarily but slightly worried.

"I . . ." Kyle started to say, then stopped. "Let's get finished packing, but then we'll have to wait for them to come back," he said reluctantly.

They both hesitated about going back into the villa. Instead of being cool and welcoming, it seemed cold. And to both of them, it seemed to be emanating a violent unsatisfied sexual hunger, straining to reach them.

They finished packing in silence and then put their packs by the big old doors, ready to leave, before going back inside. As they crossed the living area to the kitchen Mark put out a hand and stopped Kyle.

"The painting," he said, "can you see them? It's them," Mark whispered.

"I can't see anything," Kyle said, "Just the two empty chairs. I'm sorry. And I don't want to stay in here."

They quickly made toast and coffee, which they took outside to the table on the terrace. Outwardly, nothing about the villa had changed, but today the weather was cooler and the sky was overcast, and they both sat lost in their own thoughts.

"We can't wait all day," Mark suddenly exclaimed, getting up and picking up the cups and plates.

"But we can't—" Kyle started.

"Yes, we can," Mark interrupted him angrily, as he carried them inside, "You write a note explaining we had to leave. They can both read."

Then Jason and Andrew were coming in from the cobbled lane, Andrew carrying a big bag.

"Hi, what's this," Andrew cried, seeing the packs. "What are you guys up too? You can't go. We have kabobs. Got them early," he said as he plonked the bag on the table and opened it. "Fresh and hot. Hamid's uncle has a kabob shop down near the square," Andrew carried on, "And you have to stay for dinner at least. Hamid is—"

"You went out early in the morning . . . for kabobs?" Kyle interrupted.

"Yes. Hamid said they'd really be fresh and good and his uncle starts cooking them before dawn. You came in about eleven and were quiet when we left, so we didn't wake you up to tell you," he said looking at them. "We locked up and put the key under the door. Why?"

"No reason," Kyle replied, confused, and looking at Mark, who was pale.

"Hey if you guys want to go, then go," Jason said unexpectedly, moving close to them and studying their faces. "There is a pull here. I can feel it and . . . and I like it. But I'm not you guys. If it's pulling at you too, and that's not what you want, then go," he said seriously.

"Hey," Andrew interrupted, "I know the weather isn't too good today, but this place is great. There is no strange power; it's just a really cool spot. And it's only Thursday. We have the villa till next Friday. You can't leave now. Its going to be cold tonight, Hamid says, and we are going to have a wood fire inside and . . . ," he was smiling broadly at the thought of what they were going to be doing by the open fire.

"We'll leave you the car. The bus to Nicosia goes at 11.30, and we have to catch it," Mark said firmly, and he and Kyle settled their packs on their backs and left.

As they waited in the square for the bus, they saw the men and the Tree of Idleness in the Bellapais square sitting opposite them, always there, eternal, and just down the winding, uneven cobble-stoned narrow street from the ledge where the villa stood. The square leading into the Byzantine abbey forecourt. An old place Mark thought, old and full of strange primeval forces. And he shuddered as a young Turkish man looked over at them, then his friends turned their way, and they smiled, knowingly. And he felt the pull of the villa surge over him and his cock jump as he shuddered and looked away, instead fixing his eyes on Kyle and gripping his hand.

"I. . . I may not always be perfect Kyle," he said, in a husky voice, "I can't guarantee I won't ever. . . there wont ever . . ," he shrugged helplessly. "But I know I want us to last, to—"

"I'm not perfect either," Kyle interrupted, "But this is what I want too. You and me, together."

Mark and Kyle had to spend that Thursday night in a hotel before they could get a flight back to Istanbul on the next day, Friday, and then home. And at the airport the following day, they killed some time by looking through the English-language papers, and Mark picked one up, seeing a small item on one side of the front page.

Lord Cramner Dead

On Wednesday night the well known patron of the arts and literature, Valery Cramner, died peacefully at his home, Cramner House, after a very short illness. Lord Cramner, had for . . .

Chapter 9: Vincent Possession

by habu

"Don't you think it's even a little bit morbid, Jasmine, staying up here while we're attending your Grandaunt Layla's funeral?"

"I don't see why, Charles. I hadn't even ever met her son, Baris. And he didn't actually die here in the villa. He went over the wall out on the terrace there and down the cliffside. He died somewhere down there. Ahmed and Candice, could you please stop picking at each other? And, no, you can't go out on the terrace, and you can't take a swim without your father or me being there. It's not safe out there."

"Well, *I* think it's a bit morbid," Charles Vincent repeated a bit petulantly.

"Oh, come on, Charles," Jasmine said, amusement forcing out the exasperation in her voice. "You know it will be neat to be able to say you worked on your novel here in the same villa where Lawrence Durrell wrote the *Alexandria Quartet*. You just know that will impress your colleagues at in Cairo. Ahmed, I swear, if you don't stop trying to get to that terrace wall, I'm going to throw you over it myself."

She turned back to her husband. "In fact, maybe staying here will give you inspiration for another story, another book perhaps. Cousin Baris's story, for instance. I've been thinking about that. Here we are in the villa where he died, taking his own life after his secret lover, that musician Kemal whatshisname,

121

died so tragically in a car crash. I know that you might find it distasteful to write of a doomed love affair between two men, but—"

Her thought was disrupted by a squeal from out on the terrace. "Momma, Momma, Ahmed is climbing up on the wall!"

As Jasmine Vincent stormed out to the terrace of the Bellapais mountainside villa, Charles began perusing the scant collection of books on the bookcase in the villa's large living room. He saw one that intrigued him and pulled it out and started reading.

Ahh, the days of drifting down to the Tree of Idleness in the square in the late afternoon and sitting ogling the local Turkish Cypriot men and letting them ogle me until I got that certain look from one I fancied. Then taking him up to my rented villa and letting him vigorously, joyously, and noisily fuck my brains out on a lounger under the sun on the terrace overlooking the Mediterranean.

Charles was finding the words he was reading mesmerizing. He'd never heard of this book before. *The Tree of Idleness*, it was called. By some chap named Amalfi. He thumbed back to the author's notes and was surprised to read that the book was set in Bellapais, where they were, the house they were occupying both while he was on sabbatical and because Jasmine's Egyptian grandaunt Layla, who she had hardly ever met but who he regretted he'd never met, had died and would be buried in the small Anglican cemetery down in Kyrenia tomorrow afternoon. They said that Layla had died of a broken heart when her only son, Baris, threw himself off the cliffside terrace here at this very villa.

Charles regretted he'd never met Layla because the family legend was that she was the model for one of the major characters in Lawrence Durrell's acclaimed novel, *The Alexandria Quartet*. As an English professor at the American University of Cairo, Charles was steeped in the writings of Durrell, and it was quite an interesting coincidence that the Egyptian graduate student he had wooed and wed had a connection to the *Quartet*, no matter how tenuous.

Perhaps Jasmine was right, Charles mused. Perhaps it would be an interesting selling point to his own novel on modern-day Alexandria that he had written at least a portion of it while he was on sabbatical and living in the same house where Durrell had written the *Quartet*.

Charles felt an urge to read further into the Amalfi book.

And then back down to the square in the twilight after dinner with those fairy lights in the olive trees around the fringe of the stone café terrace, and, in that soft light and twittering laughter of the Mediterranean men and wisps of strong Turkish tobacco drifting up, eyeing and being eyed until I got the certain look from one I fancied and took him back up to the villa and let him fuck me in long, slow, sweeping strokes on the terrace under the stars.

And maybe, if he was really, really beautiful and masterful, taking him back to my bed for a night of sleep broken by brief periods of wanton lust, waking to the feel of a hot poker at my hole and a wheedling whisper for permission at my ear and arching back to accept the homage of a throbbing need to be deep inside me. Breakfasting on the terrace by the small pool and then pulling him into the pool and wrapping my legs around his waist and letting the swirling water soften the rhythmic in and outing as I threw my head back and watched the morning Mediterranean light filter through the sighing branches of the olive trees and thought about my late afternoon visit to the Tree of Idleness café in the Bellapais square, already assessing which eyes I would respond to today.

The light was dimming and the children had had their swim and Jasmine had fed them their dinner and Charles was still sitting at the writing desk, in the darkening living room, reading from the Amalfi book. Whenever he lifted his head, his eyes went to the strange painting over the desk. It was marked with the signature of the famous British painter, Valery Cramner, who had recently died, but surely such a valuable painting wouldn't be here in a rental villa. Would it? It was such a sad, haunting painting, devoid of life, even though the colors of the empty café chairs in front of the sun-sparkling stone wall were luminous. And then his attention to go to the house itself. He felt the very walls of the villa murmuring to him, humming in a singsong tune to return his attention to the book.

Charles had had feelings for other men before—the feelings that the almost poetic prose of the Amalfi book was infusing him with—but he'd been far too sensible to pursue any of them. He wanted tenure at the university. In Egypt that required a straight-laced life and publication. He was quite fond of Jasmine, and he worshipped their children. And that was enough for him. Or it had been enough for him before they had come up here to Bellapais. Reading this Amalfi chap's book, though, was getting his juices going, surfacing urges in him that he hadn't had since his undergraduate days.

"It's time to go down to Kyrenia, Charles," Jasmine was saying. She was standing by the desk. She had intruded into the murmuring of the walls around Charles, and he resented the intrusion. It seemed like the very walls of the villa were indignant at the intrusion—and the Amalfi book was as well. There seemed to be a tension gripping the villa at the mere presence of a woman and children. The maleness of the place permeated the villa.

"Umm, um," Charles responded, returning his eyes to the text. He scooted a bit further under the desk, not wanting Jasmine to see that he was sexually aroused.

"It's dark now," Jasmine was saying in the wheedling voice of hers when she was a bit on edge. "And you know we are spending the night down at my grandaunt's Kyrenia house in preparation for the funeral tomorrow."

Charles looked up, glassy-eyed, trying to focus. "Perhaps you and the children could go on down yourselves for the night, honey," he offered. "You know, I have some ideas running through my head. Some very important elements of the novel. Perhaps it would be good for me to stay here tonight and work on the writing. You know, without any distractions at all. It might be just what I need to jump start this."

Jasmine was torn. Charles had been slow in getting the novel started. She'd done everything she could to goose that along. Charles needed this to get tenure. The family needed Charles to get tenure.

Charles waited until he was quite sure that Jasmine and the children were on the road down to Kyrenia. He knew exactly what to do then. The walls were murmuring to him; the Amalfi

124

book had practically dropped in his lap. He'd been hard since he had opened the book and started reading those passages. He hadn't been this hard and jittery and full of the electricity of lust and anticipation since his undergraduate days. He even could hear the sounds from the square below. The activity at the Tree of Idleness down in the Bellapais square. The sounds of men's voices and of the baglama playing. There's no reason he should hear those sounds up here on the mountainside above the square. But he did.

Charles went into the bedroom and stripped down. He then pulled on a tight T-shirt and those jeans Jasmine insisted were two sizes too small for him—without briefs under them. He stood back and looked at himself in the mirror. Yes, the outline at his basket was quite discernible. He knew he was good looking, but he also knew the size of him was his most attracting feature. He was humming as he descended the steep cobble-stoned pathway toward the welcoming, twinkling fairy lights laced through the spreading Tree of Idleness in the square below and toward the sound in the outdoor café of male laughter and raunchy bravado.

Authors' Notes

The setting of this novel, the historical casting of Cyprus during the 1958–2008 period covered by the narrative as well as the villa itself on the mountainside in the upper reaches of the Cypriot ancient abbey village of Bellapais, is real, as are the Tree of Idleness café in the Bellapais square, the British author Lawrence Durrell and his celebrated *The Alexandria Quartet* and *Bitter Lemons*. Both books were, in fact, penned while Durrell lived in the Bellapais villa between 1953 and 1957. One of this novel's authors, habu, also lived in the villa and penned novels there in the mid 1990s. The character of Layla is also based on a real person.

Beyond this foundation, the events and characters are fictional, as is the novel, *The Tree of Idleness*, which is attributed to Mark Amalfi. The inspiration for this novel comes from a writing exercise entered into by the two authors, who are amalgamated here into the author Shabbu: habu, who lives on the East Coast of the United States, and sabb, who lives on the East Coast of the Australia. The two have met in cyber space to spin stories together. The exercise set here was to use the same three-paragraph passage in stories by each of the authors and by the two combined and then to weave them into a coherent work using, to a limited extent, literary devices woven so skillfully by Lawrence Durrell in the *The Alexandria Quartet*.

These include the weaving of subplots with minor characters throughout the series of separate stories that are able to stand on their own as stories, multiple intertwined and doomed love relationships, the major plotlines being twisted as stories unfold, and the resolution of selected threads in one story occurring in separate stories. We hope that we have both succeeded to some extent in this exercise and entertained the reader in the process.

About the Authors

Shabbu is the combined pen name for two established authors, one on the East Coast of the United States and one on the East Coast of Australia, who spin erotica together in cyber space.

Habu, a bisexual former supersonic spy jet pilot, intelligence agent, and diplomat, is a published mainstream novelist and short story writer under another name and in another dimension of his life.

Sabb, once an accountant and sometime property developer, is a wild barbarian at heart, who knows that love is out there of you're lucky enough to find it.

You can find them at www.BarbarianSpy.com. These authors' erotic, and nonerotic, e-novels and anthologies are published by BarbarianSpy in e-book and paperback, and available from www.BarbarianSpy.com or at all major on-line book retailers. Habu is also published by eXcessica LLC.

Our authors like to receive feedback and to have reviews of their work posted to www.goodreads.com and other review sites.

Barbarian Spy

FOR LITERARY HEAT

Not all books listed below may currently be on release.
* indicates the book is available in paperback and e-book.

BOOKS BY DIRK HESSIAN

Xtreme Erotica
The King's Men
Shores of Tripoli
Prophecy of Noto
Pretender's Fate

General Erotica/Romance
Fire Down the Valley*
Constantinople*
The Beautiful Way*
Blue and Gray
Colonel's Treasure
Beginning of Time
Labyrinth

BOOKS BY HABU

Gay Erotica
Memoir Faction
Flying High, Diving Deep*
Xtreme Erotica
Apyko: The Greek Pimp
Visits of the Schlange
Second Coming: Emile La Cour Unleashed
Vortex: Sacrificed by Curiosity*
Dark Angel Sounding *(in e-book & included in
Sounding:Ultimate Control Paperback)**
Sounding: Ultimate Control (*Print Only*)*
Sounding Five *(in e-book & included in
Sounding:Ultimate Control paperback)**
General Erotica
Romance
Snowy, Snowy Nights (Christmas Romance)

Four Coins
Lower Than the Heart
Brambleton
Gotta Keep Trying
Finding Amnad
Platres Conclave
Other Novels/Novellas
Cruising Gigolo
Prepared in Cape Verdi
Gilded Cage
House on Park
Anything for Ambition
Dance of the Ravishers
Hard Knocks U*
My Neighbor's Spa*
Man's Man: Tales of a High Priced Gay Hooker*
Trip Money
Clint Folsom Mysteries Compendium Volume 1*
Death to Blonds - Stolen Judgment (Clint Folsom
Mystery)*
Clint Folsom Mysteries Compendium Volume 2*
The Indian Doctor
Sailorboy
Home to Fire Island
Choke Hold
Gay Erotica Anthologies
Spy Tales 001*
Spy Tales 002*
Doubled*
Doubled Again*
Tails in the Tropics*
Tails in the Med*
Tails in the West*
Rough Riders*
Grab Bag 1*
Grab Bag 2*
Grab Bag 3*
Grab Bag 4*

Grab Bag 5*
Beyond the Beaded Curtain*
Habu's Christmas Balls
The Sporting Life*
Fetish Galore!*
Literary Gay Erotica
Cairo Surrender*
The Handyman*
Homeward Bound
Journey to Mirage*
Menage Erotica
Cruising Gigolo
13 Ways for Halloween
Luther*
The Indian Prince
Literary GLBT Fiction
Summer of Denial
BOOKS BY SHABBU
Finding Jason
Dirty Pool
Operation Black Jade
Cigars!*
Angel in the Barn
Gayly Complicated*
Despoiling David
The Tree of Idleness*
I Met a Man
The Interview
Rough Road to Happiness
BOOKS BY SABB
Hiring in Hollywood
The Legend of Holleystone Grange
Surprise Encounters
She is He
Wrong Man
Loyal to his King
Barbarian Tales - Book One - Traveler's Tales*
Barbarian Tales - Book Two - Journeys Begin*

Barbarian Tales - Book Three - The Inheritance*
Barbarian Tales - Book Four - Road to Persepolis*

www.ingramcontent.com/pod-product-compliance
Lightning Source LLC
Chambersburg PA
CBHW021923170626
46807CB00007B/2960